The car door opened and Alesia was ushered into the nightclub amidst an explosion of flashbulbs and photographers yelling for her to look this way and that. One photographer came in too close and was instantly blocked by two of Sebastien's security team.

Alesia glanced around her in confusion and astonishment. 'I can't think why they're suddenly so interested in me,' she muttered, and Sebastien flashed her a seductive smile that seriously threatened her ability to walk in a straight line.

'Because I married you, *agape mou*,' he drawled lazily, 'and our two families have been at war for three generations. Newspaper editors are loving it, and so are the gossip magazines. Photographs of us will sell for a small fortune.'

She gaped at him. If only they knew what she knew—that their marriage was a sham!

SALE OR
RETURN BRIDE

BY
SARAH MORGAN

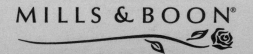

First published in Great Britain 2005
Harlequin Mills & Boon Limited,
Eton House, 18-24 Paradise Road, Richmond, Surrey TW9 1SR

© Sarah Morgan 2005

ISBN 0 263 84187 1

Set in Times Roman 10¼ on 11½ pt.
01-1005-53570

Printed and bound in Spain
by Litografia Rosés, S.A., Barcelona

CHAPTER ONE

'Sebastien Fiorukis?' Alesia gaped at her grandfather, the grandfather who had been a stranger to her in all but reputation for her whole life. 'In exchange for the money I need, you expect me to marry *Sebastien Fiorukis*?'

'Precisely.' Alesia's grandfather smiled an unpleasant smile as she struggled to find her voice and fought to control the torrent of emotion that surged up inside her. Whatever she'd expected when she'd been working up the courage to tackle her grandfather, it hadn't been that.

Fiorukis. The Greek tycoon who had taken his father's moderately successful business and built it into a corporation that rivalled that of her grandfather; the billionaire reputed to be every bit as ruthless as her grandfather; the man who moved between women at a speed faster than the cars he drove and the jets he flew. The man who—

'You can't be serious!' She looked up, her teeth gritted and her eyes stinging. The very thought made her feel *sick*. 'The Fiorukis family was responsible for the death of my father—'

And she despised them as much as she despised her grandfather.

As much as she despised everything Greek.

'And because of that, my blood-line died out,' her grandfather said harshly. 'Now I shall ensure the same fate for the Fiorukis family. If he marries you then it will end with the son, just as mine did.'

Alesia stopped breathing, rigid with shock. *He knew.*

Somehow he knew.

The file she was holding dropped from her nerveless fin-

5

gers and papers scattered across the marble floor. She didn't notice.

As the full implication of his words sank into her shocked brain, her face paled and her voice was little more than a whisper. 'You know that I can't have children—?'

How could he know? How could he be party to such an intimate, personal detail?

All her life she'd kept that information private. The only slight salve to her pain had been that her anguish was her own—*that no one would pity her.*

She stared at him, her breathing rapid. She'd arrived strong and full of purpose. Now suddenly she felt vulnerable and exposed. Stripped naked in front of a man who, despite their shared blood-line, had been a stranger from her childhood.

That man was watching her now, an expression of smug satisfaction in his hard eyes.

Her grandfather, Dimitrios Philipos.

'I make it my business to know everything about everyone.' His tone was brittle and unsympathetic as he observed her distress with evident satisfaction. 'Information is the key to success in life.'

Alesia swallowed back the lump building in her throat. How could such personal agony ever be considered 'success'?

Marriage.

It was the cruellest taunt. She'd long ago been forced to come to terms with the fact that, no matter what her future held, it wouldn't be marriage. How could it? How could a woman in her position ever marry?

Her mind raced ahead, trying to keep up with the evil genius of her grandfather. 'If you *truly* know everything about me then you must also know the reason I'm here. You must know that my mother is getting sicker, that she needs an operation—'

His smile was unpleasant. 'Let's just say I've been expecting you. You didn't disappoint me.'

Fury shot through her, driving out the weakness induced by his reminder of her own limitations as a woman.

She hated him.

Alesia stared at the grandfather she'd never even met before this moment and gave a shiver of revulsion. Her head throbbed with a tension headache that had been plaguing her since she'd stepped off the plane at Athens Airport and she felt a dull ache in the pit of her stomach, a reminder that she'd been too nervous to eat for the past few days.

So much was at stake. Her mother's future lay in her hands, in her ability to negotiate some sort of deal with a man who was nothing short of a monster.

He presided over the room like a king, seated in an enormous gilded chair with ornately curved handles, barking out orders to terrified staff who hovered within shouting distance.

Alesia glanced around the opulent room with distaste. Such a blatant display of wealth sickened her.

Did the man have no shame? Did he know that she held down three jobs in order to give her mother the care that she needed?

Care that *he* should have been providing for the past fifteen years.

Alesia took a deep breath and tried to calm herself. Temper would get her nowhere. It took enormous effort not to just turn and walk from the room, leaving the old man to his piles of money and lonely existence. But she couldn't do that. She had to ignore the fact that he was the most selfish, shallow individual she'd ever laid eyes on and she had to ignore the fact that if it hadn't been for her mother she wouldn't be standing here now. She had to stay focused on the task in hand.

Nothing—*nothing*—was going to distract her from her reason for being here. He'd ignored her mother's needs for fifteen years, denied her very existence, but Alesia wasn't going to let him ignore *her*. Not any longer. It was time that he remembered what family was supposed to be about.

'Wipe that expression off your face. You came to me, remember? You're the one who wants the money.' Dimitrios's voice was harsh and heavily accented and Alesia stiffened defensively.

'For my mother.'

He gave a grunt of contempt. 'She could have asked me herself if she had any backbone.'

Alesia felt the anger rise inside her again and squashed it down with ruthless determination. She sensed that if she let her emotions rule then he'd show her the door. 'My mother is very unwell—'

He watched her closely, a nasty smile on his face. 'And that's the only reason you're here, isn't it? Nothing else would induce you to step over my threshold. You hate me. She's taught you to hate me.' He leaned forward. 'You're furiously angry and you're trying to hide it because you don't want to risk antagonizing me in case I say no. In case I slam the lid of my coffer shut and catch your fingers.'

He threw back his head and laughed, obviously enjoying the situation enormously.

Refusing to believe that anyone could be so totally lacking in conscience, Alesia spread her hands and tried to appeal to his sense of reason. 'She was *your son's wife*—'

'Don't remind me.' The laughter faded and he sat back in his chair watching her without a flicker of remorse or regret. 'It's a shame you weren't a boy. You look as though you've inherited his spirit. You even look a little like him, apart from that blonde hair and those blue eyes. You should have had dark hair and dark eyes and if my son hadn't been seduced by that woman you would have had the pedigree you deserve and you wouldn't have lived the last fifteen years of your life in exile. All this could have been yours.'

Alesia glanced round the room at 'all this'. The contrast between her own circumstances and those of her grandfather couldn't have been more marked. Evidence of his wealth was everywhere, from the ostentatious statues that guarded the entrance of virtually every doorway in his mansion to the enormous fountain that gushed forth in the elaborate courtyard.

Alesia thought of her own home in a rough area of London—a small ground-floor flat which she'd had converted to accommodate her mother's disability—all that she could afford after she'd paid for the help her mother needed.

Then she thought of her mother and her long struggle for survival. *A struggle which this man could have lessened.*

She gritted her teeth and doubled the effort required not to walk from the room. 'I'm perfectly happy with my pedigree,' she said stiffly, 'and I love England.'

'Don't answer me back!' He turned on her with an enraged growl and for a moment she tensed, sure that he was going to hit her. 'If you answer back, he'll never marry you. You may not look Greek but I want your behaviour to be totally Greek. You will be meek and obedient and you will not venture an opinion on any subject unless asked. *Do you hear me?*'

Alesia stared at him in disbelief. 'You're serious about this? You really think I'm going to marry a Fiorukis?'

Her grandfather gave an ugly smile. 'If you want the money, then yes. You'll marry Sebastien Fiorukis and you'll make sure he doesn't find out about your infertility. I will make sure that the terms of the deal will tie him to you in marriage until you produce an heir. Seeing as you will never produce an heir, then he will be locked in a childless marriage for ever, unable to extract himself.' Dimitrios Philipos threw back his head and gave a nasty laugh. 'The perfect retribution. They always say that revenge is a dish best eaten cold. I've waited fifteen years for this moment but it was

worth the wait. It's masterly. You are the tool of my revenge.'

Alesia stared at him in undisguised horror, so shocked by
his vindictive plan that she was unable to hide her distaste.

No wonder her mother had warned her that the man was
evil. He didn't have an ounce of compassion in his body.

'I can't do that.' She lifted a hand to her throat. Suddenly
she couldn't breathe. The room was totally airless. 'You can't
ask me to do that.'

She couldn't marry Sebastien Fiorukis. He had all the characteristics she despised in a man. To be asked to spend her
life with him—

Alesia closed her eyes and tried to remember how she'd
got into this situation. She'd never believed in feuds and
vengeance.

She was English!

Her grandfather's smile was unpleasant. 'If you want the
money then you'll do it.'

Alesia bit her lip hard, her mind racing in all directions.

She wanted the money. *She had to have the money.* 'It's
wrong—'

'It's justice,' her grandfather said, his voice icy-cold. 'Justice that we should have meted out to the Fiorukis family a
long time ago. The Greek always avenge their dead and you,
even though you are only *half* Greek, should know this.'

Alesia stared at him helplessly.

Was this the time to tell him that she hated everything
Greek? *That she didn't feel at all Greek and never would?*

She stayed silent, she couldn't risk alienating her grandfather.

Anything.

That was what she'd told herself before she'd arrived at
her grandfather's villa today. She'd do *anything* to get the
money she needed.

But she'd underestimated her grandfather's ability to turn her desperation to his own advantage.

She studied him carefully, noting the chill in his eyes and the ugly set of his fleshy mouth. The thought flashed through her brain that to intentionally make an enemy of this man would be foolish in the extreme. Then she almost laughed at her own naïvety. They were enemies already. Had been from the day that her mother had smiled up at her father and captured his heart, shattering Dimitrios's plans for a wedding to a good Greek girl.

'Fiorukis will never agree to marry me,' she said calmly. 'He'll refuse.'

And then she wouldn't have to spend the rest of her life with a man she'd been bred to hate. There was no way he'd agree to marry her, she consoled herself. Sebastien Fiorukis discarded women with ruthless efficiency and with a casual disregard for their feelings. It was common knowledge that marriage was right at the bottom of his agenda.

Why would he marry *her*, when their families were virtually at war?

'Sebastien Fiorukis is first and foremost a businessman,' her grandfather said in derisive tones, 'and the inducement I have offered him to marry my granddaughter will prove too tempting for him to pass up.'

'What inducement?'

Her grandfather gave a nasty smile. 'Let's just say that I have something he wants—which is the basis of all successful business negotiations. He is also a man who can't pass an attractive woman and not make a move on her. For some reason he favours blonde women, so you're in luck—or you will be once we've got you out of those tatty jeans and dressed you in something decent. And if you want that money then you won't do anything to put him off. Now clear up the mess you made on my floor.'

In luck? Her grandfather truly thought that attracting the attentions of that arrogant, ruthless Greek was lucky?

Functioning on automatic, Alesia stooped and gathered together the papers with shaking hands, her mind working quickly. What choice did she have? There was no other possible source for the money she needed. If there had been then she wouldn't be standing here now. And it wouldn't be marriage in the true sense of the word. They probably wouldn't even need to speak to each other very often—

'If I do it—if I say yes, you'll give me the money?'

'No—' her grandfather gave a grunt '—but Fiorukis will. It will be part of the agreement. He will give you an allowance every month. How you spend that will be up to you.'

Alesia's mouth fell open. Her grandfather had managed to construct a deal where he didn't even have to part with his money—

Sebastien Fiorukis was not only going to have to marry the granddaughter of his greatest enemy but he was going to have to pay for the privilege.

Why would he agree to such an outrageous idea?

What exactly was the inducement that her grandfather had referred to?

She raised a shaking hand to her temple, wishing that her head would stop aching. Wishing that she could think clearly.

She knew enough about her grandfather to assume that, for whatever reason, Sebastien Fiorukis would agree to the deal.

Which meant that if she wanted the money then she was going to have to do the one thing she'd promised herself that she'd never do.

She was going to have to marry.

And marry not just anyone, but the man whose family had been responsible for the death of her father.

A man she hated.

*   *   *

'Why would Dimitrios Philipos come to us?' Sebastien Fiorukis paced the terrace that ran the length of his luxury Athenian villa and then paused to study his father, his handsome face devoid of expression. He'd learned at an early age the advantage of inscrutability and he practised the art to perfection. 'The feud between our families goes back for three generations.'

'Apparently that's the reason for his approach,' Leandros Fiorukis said cautiously. 'He thinks it's time to mend fences. Publicly.'

'Mend fences?' Sebastien raised an eyebrow, incredulity lighting his expressive dark eyes. 'Since when did Dimitrios Philipos ever want to mend fences? The man is evil and totally without conscience.'

The fact that his father was even *considering* meeting with the man astonished him. But his father was growing old, Sebastien acknowledged with a tinge of regret, and the loss of the family company so many years earlier had been a thorn in his side for too long.

His father sighed. 'I want this feud to end, Sebastien. I want to retire in peace with your mother, knowing that what is rightfully ours has been returned. I no longer have the stomach for a fight.'

At the prospect of finally going head to head with his lifelong enemy, Sebastien gave a dangerous smile. Fortunately he had no such reservations. In fact he positively thrived on confrontation and animosity. If Dimitrios Philipos thought that he could play his usual game of bullying and intimidation then he was going to discover that he'd finally met his match.

His father picked up some papers. 'The deal he is offering is astonishing.'

'All the more reason to be suspicious of his motives,' Sebastien drawled in cool tones and Leandros Fiorukis eyed his son cautiously.

'You would be a fool not to listen and I know you're not a fool,' his father said carefully. 'Whatever else he may be, Dimitrios Philipos is still a Greek. He pays you a compliment by offering to meet.'

'The day Dimitrios Philipos pays me a compliment is the day I reach for a weapon,' Sebastien drawled lazily, his gaze lingering on his father's face, registering the lines of worry and the dark shadows.

Suddenly he realized that his father had aged. That the strain of the ongoing feud had been too much for him.

'I have agreed to the meeting on your behalf—' His father looked at him wearily and Sebastien gritted his teeth and vowed that, whatever it took, he would end this feud once and for all, even if he had to take Philipos down with his bare hands.

'Good.' His tone was curt. 'It's time to end this. Tell me what he's offering.'

'He's returning your birthright. He's handing over his company.' His father gave a harsh laugh and dropped the papers on to the table. 'Or should I say "our company" since that is how it started out before Philipos defrauded your grandfather?'

Philipos was offering back the company? Sebastien hid his shock, his dark eyes veiled as he watched his father. *It couldn't be that easy.* 'And in return?'

His father's gaze slid from his. 'You marry his grand-daughter.'

'You're joking!' Stunning dark eyes alight with incredulity and more than a trace of amusement, Sebastien stared at his father in disbelief. 'What century are we in?'

Without meeting his gaze, his father shuffled the papers in front of him. 'Unfortunately those are his terms.'

Sebastien stilled. 'You're *not* joking.' The humour faded from his tone and suddenly his voice was lethally soft. 'In which case you ought to know that I can't think of anyone who would be less appealing as a potential consort than a blood relative of Philipos.'

His father lifted a hand and rubbed the back of his neck to relieve the tension. 'You are thirty-four, Sebastien. At some point you have to marry someone. Unless you wish to spend your life alone and childless.'

'I want children,' Sebastien said flatly, 'very much. It's the wife that gives me a problem. Unfortunately I require certain qualities in a woman that don't appear to exist.'

He thought about the extremely beautiful gymnast he'd spent the last few evenings with. And before that the dancer. None of them held his attention for more than a few weeks at a time.

'Well, if you can't marry for love, then why not for sound business reasons?' his father said gruffly. 'If you marry the girl, the company is ours.'

Sebastien's mind was racing at speed. 'That's it?' His eyes narrowed. 'It can't be that simple.'

His father relaxed slightly, his expression suddenly hopeful. 'He's an old man. The company is in trouble. There are few men skilled enough to sort out the problems and Philipos knows that you are one of them. Even he acknowledges that you are a brilliant businessman. By insisting on the marriage he ensures that his granddaughter will be financially secure in the event that the company folds. And it won't with you at the helm. It's a generous offer.'

'That's what concerns me,' Sebastien drawled softly. 'Dimitrios Philipos is not renowned for his generous offers.'

'He is offering a considerable inducement to marry the girl.'

'I'd need a considerable inducement to agree to marry a woman that I haven't ever laid eyes on,' Sebastien said tightly, his razor-sharp brain working quickly.

Why would Philipos be offering him the company?

And why would he want him to marry his granddaughter?

His father looked at him wearily. 'It's time to put aside suspicion and learn to trust. Philipos started that business with my father and then took it from him. He claims that he regrets the past and wants to put it right before he dies.'

Sebastien stilled, his mind racing ahead, asking one key question. *Why?* 'And you believe him?'

His father shrugged. 'Our lawyers are in possession of a draft agreement as we speak. What reason do I have not to believe him?'

'Perhaps because Dimitrios Philipos is an evil megalo-maniac who only ever acts in his own interests,' Sebastien said caustically, wrenching the silk tie away from his neck and dropping it over the nearest chair. He felt the tension rise inside him. Suddenly the stakes were high and he felt the familiar rush of adrenalin. The higher the stakes the more satisfaction was to be gained by playing. 'Do I really need to remind you of his sins towards our family?'

'He's an old man. Perhaps he's repenting.'

Sebastien threw back his head and laughed but his dark eyes glittered dangerously. 'Repent? The old bastard wouldn't know the meaning of the word. I'm almost tempted to go along with the idea just to see what game he's playing this time.' Sebastien undid the top two buttons of his shirt and gestured to one of his discreetly hovering staff to bring drinks. The heat in Athens in July was punishing. 'So why can't the granddaughter find her own husband? Philipos certainly keeps her existence quiet. No one ever sees or hears of her. Is she just ugly or does she have some vile disease that would be passed on to my offspring?'

'They would be her offspring too,' his father pointed out, 'and you haven't managed to find a wife.'

'I haven't been looking for a wife,' Sebastien said silkily, 'and I certainly don't need one hand-picked by my greatest enemy.'

The thought almost had him laughing. There was little

doubt in his mind that the Philipos heiress must have some *very* unfortunate traits or she would have been married long before now.

'I'm sure she's a lovely girl,' his father muttered and Sebastien lifted a dark eyebrow in mockery.

'On the contrary, I am expecting her to have two heads and no personality. If she *were* lovely then Philipos wouldn't hide her away and the press would have tracked her the way they track me. She is, after all, an extremely wealthy young woman.'

'The press track you because you give them plenty to write about,' his father said dryly, 'whereas the Philipos heiress has been in England.'

'And England has the most intrusive tabloid press of all,' Sebastien murmured, a frown touching his handsome features. 'Which makes the situation even more interesting. If they have left her alone then she undoubtedly has two heads and no personality.'

His father sighed in exasperation. 'Evidently she leads a discreet life. Unlike you. The girl went to an English boarding school. Her mother was English, if you remember.'

'Of course I remember.' Sebastien drained his glass, vivid memories clouding his brain. 'I also remember that she was killed when our boat exploded. Along with her husband, who was Dimitrios Philipos's only son.' Memories flickered across his brain... *A child, limp and lifeless in his arms as he dragged her to the surface of the water; chaos, blood, people screaming...* Sebastien gritted his teeth. 'She lost both her parents and Philipos blames us for their deaths. And now he wants me to marry his granddaughter?' He lifted an eyebrow, his expression sardonic. 'Given her genealogy, I will have to sleep with a dagger under my pillow. I'm amazed that you accept the suggestion with such equanimity.'

'We too lost family in that explosion,' his father said

heavily. 'And time has passed. Enough time. He's an old man.'

'He's an evil man.'

'We were not responsible for his son's death. Perhaps time has given him the opportunity to reflect and he realizes that now.' Leandros ran his fingers over his brow, visibly disturbed by the memories of that terrible time. 'He wants her to have a Greek husband. He wants his line rebuilt.'

Sebastien narrowed his eyes and wondered when his father had grown so soft. If Philipos wanted his half-English granddaughter to have a Greek husband then there was undoubtedly a reason. *And he intended to discover that reason.*

'What about the girl? Why would she agree to such a marriage? She is the granddaughter of Dimitrios Philipos. As such she is unlikely to be possessed of the emotional stability I would want in a wife.'

'At least meet her.' His father tried a different approach. 'You can always say no.'

Sebastien surveyed him thoughtfully. It was true that he wanted children. And he'd always wanted to restore Philipos Industries to his family, where it belonged.

'What is in it for her?' His voice was sharp. 'Philipos gets his grandchild, I gain a son and a company that is rightfully ours—what does she gain?'

His father hesitated and shuffled the papers in front of him. 'Sebastien—'

Sebastien inhaled sharply. '*Tell* me.'

His father glanced at him warily. 'On the day of your wedding you are to pay money into her personal account.' He shifted awkwardly as he studied the papers again. 'A substantial sum. That sum is to be repeated every month during your marriage.'

There was a long silence. Then Sebastien gave a disbelieving laugh. 'Are you seriously telling me that the Philipos heiress wants *money* for marrying me?'

'The financial settlement is an important part of the deal.'

'The woman is already richer than Midas himself,' Sebastien launched, his volatile Mediterranean temperament rising to the surface with the force of an erupting volcano. 'And yet she wants *more*?'

His father cleared his throat. 'The terms of the deal are very clear. She receives money.'

Sebastien strode to the edge of the terrace and stared down across the city he loved so deeply.

'Sebastien—'

He turned quickly, the expression in his dark eyes cynical and hard. 'Why do I even hesitate?' He shrugged broad shoulders in a dismissive gesture. 'All women are gold-diggers, the fact that this one chooses to dig deeper than most changes nothing. At least she is honest about it, which is to her credit. As you rightly say, this is a business arrangement where both parties understand the score.'

'You make her sound hard and money-grabbing but why not reserve judgement?' his father urged. He looked at his son helplessly. 'Any relative of Philipos is going to be accustomed to an extremely extravagant lifestyle. Her requirement for funds may not be a reflection on her character. She might be sweet.'

Sebastien winced and refrained from pointing out that his taste didn't run to 'sweet' girls. 'Sweet girls don't demand huge sums of money from prospective husbands. And if she's a Philipos then she will have horns and a tail,' he said drily. 'And I'll do well to remember not to turn my back on her.'

'Sebastien—'

'Like you, I want the business restored to the family, so I'll see her because I'm intrigued. But I'm making no promises,' Sebastien warned grimly, depositing his empty glass on the table. 'If she's to be the mother of my children then I at least have to be able to stomach the sight of her.'

*   *   *

'You are not to speak.' Dimitrios Philipos glared at Alesia as the helicopter hovered over the landing pad. 'And you are to keep those flashing eyes of yours fixed on the ground. You are to be meek and obedient like a good Greek girl. If you keep your mouth shut until the wedding takes place, everything will be fine. By then it will be too late for Fiorukis to change his mind.'

At that precise moment Alesia was more concerned with her own state of mind than that of her prospective groom.

Why did they have to visit him on his private island? What was wrong with the mainland?

Satisfying herself that the helicopter was safely down, Alesia relaxed her death grip on her seat and forced herself to draw some much-needed oxygen into her starving lungs. Even the supposed safety of the helicopter hadn't distracted her from the vast expanse of azure-blue ocean beneath them. She was terrified of the water and always had been. And she still couldn't believe that she'd actually agreed to this meeting.

Suddenly she felt terrified. Terrified that her hatred of her grandfather would show along with her contempt for the entire Fiorukis family. 'What if he knows that I can't have children?'

If her grandfather had discovered that the childhood accident had left her unable to bear children, then how did she know that Sebastien Fiorukis hadn't discovered the same thing?

'He doesn't know. Until recently he didn't even know of your existence. He will never know until you are safely married and he discovers that you are unable to provide him with a son.' Dimitrios Philipos gave a nasty smile and Alesia flinched.

This was all wrong.

She shouldn't be doing this.

And then she remembered the money. She *had* to have

that money. She would do anything for that money. And anyway, was what she was doing really so bad? If Sebastien Fiorukis was a gentle, decent man then it would have been different and her strong sense of right and wrong would never have allowed her to go ahead with a wedding, knowing what she knew. But he wasn't like that.

The whole Fiorukis family was every bit as corrupt as her grandfather and Sebastien was at the helm. From what she'd heard, he was Greek to the very core. He was utterly without conscience and as cold and ruthless as her grandfather. Judging from his total lack of interest in commitment, he'd never had any great desire to become a father. Undoubtedly he would be a terrible father. To give a man like that an innocent child would be wrong. Perhaps it would be a good thing for everyone if both lines ended, she thought grimly. Philipos and Fiorukis. At least the feud would be buried with them.

And both men owed her. Between them they were responsible for the accident that had wrecked her family. It was time for them to pay.

On the day of the wedding, Fiorukis would transfer a lump sum into her account and continue to do so for the remainder of their marriage. Which meant that her mother could have the operation she so desperately needed. No more worries, no more holding down three jobs and worrying that the money wouldn't stretch.

As long as Fiorukis didn't discover that her mother was still alive.

Alesia bit her lip. If he found *that* out then it wouldn't take a man of his intelligence two minutes to realize that her grandfather had no love for her whatsoever and that this entire deal was suspicious.

She paused in the doorway of the helicopter and gave a soft gasp as the heat thumped into her. It was on the tip of her tongue to ask her grandfather how, if she was truly half

Greek, she found the heat so intolerable but she held the words back. Over the past few days she'd learned that the best way of dealing with her grandfather was to stay silent.

'Don't forget.' Her grandfather jerked her back roughly and glared at her. 'You are now a Philipos.'

Alesia hid her distaste. 'You refused to let my mother use that name,' she said thickly, 'but now, when it suits you, you expect *me* to use it.'

'Fiorukis is to marry you because you're a Philipos,' he reminded her with an evil smile. 'If he knew you were a nobody he wouldn't touch you with a bargepole. And stop tugging at that dress.'

Alesia gritted her teeth and released her grip on the hemline. 'It is positively indecent. It barely covers anything.'

'Precisely.' Her grandfather glanced over her and gave a satisfied grunt. 'A man likes to know what he's buying. Remember everything I said. Fiorukis has a brain as sharp as the business end of a razor but he's still a red-blooded Greek. One look at you in that and he won't be thinking business, I can assure you. You wear the dress as if you dress like that every day. You do not mention the existence of your mother. You do not say *why* you want the money.'

'He'll want to know why I'm marrying him,' Alesia said defiantly and her grandfather gave an unpleasant smile.

'Sebastien Fiorukis has an ego as large as Greece. And for some unfathomable reason women can't seem to leave him alone. Probably because he's rich and good-looking and women are usually too stupid to resist that combination.' Her grandfather gave a snort of derision. 'He'll assume you're just another in a long line of admirers who want access to his millions.'

Alesia shuddered. The man must be arrogant beyond belief. To be considered so brainless and shallow as to judge a man by his looks and his wallet seemed to her the ultimate insult. 'I don't think—'

'Good!' Her grandfather glared at her as he interrupted her stammered protest. 'I don't want you to think. And neither does he. You are not required to think. You are merely required to lie down for him whenever he pleases. And if he asks you, then you desire this marriage simply because Sebastien Fiorukis is one of the most eligible bachelors in the world and you are keen to rediscover your Greek roots. And try not to flash those eyes at him. A Greek man does not like confrontation in the marriage bed.'

Marriage bed?

Alesia felt her stomach lurch. Somehow she'd managed to avoid thinking about the deeper implications of this marriage. That they would have to become physically intimate. But then she remembered everything she'd read about Sebastien Fiorukis. If reports were correct, then he had at least three mistresses on the go at once. Given his complete lack of interest in commitment, he was hardly likely to weld himself to her bed, was he? He'd be a wandering husband and that suited her perfectly. As long as he deposited the right amount of money in her account every month, she'd be more than happy never to lay eyes on the man.

She swayed slightly and, if it hadn't been for her grandfather urging her forward down the steps, she would have backed into the helicopter and begged the pilot to take them back to the mainland.

As it was she was forced to take those few steps on to the Tarmac, forced to blink in the dazzling sunlight, dimly aware of a powerful figure watching her from a safe distance.

The situation suddenly overwhelmed her and she would have paused again had her grandfather not pushed her hard. Unprepared for the unexpected force of that push and unused to wearing such ridiculously high heels, she would have lost her balance had strong arms not reached out and steadied her.

Shocked and embarrassed, Alesia gasped out her thanks,

her fingers curling into rock-hard biceps as she tried to regain her balance. A dark male face swam in front of her and for a brief moment she collided with night-black eyes. A strange sensation curled deep in her pelvis and she felt the colour seep into her cheeks.

'Miss Philipos?'

It took a moment for Alesia to realize that he was addressing her because the name was so unfamiliar.

'Stand up, girl!' Her grandfather's impatient tones cut through her thoughts. 'A man can't stand a woman who clings. And for goodness' sake speak when you're spoken to! What was the point of that expensive education if you can't even string a sentence together?'

Her face hot with embarrassment and humiliation, Alesia regained her balance and cast an agonized glance at her rescuer. 'I'm sorry, I—'

'No apology is needed.' Sebastien spoke in cool, measured tones but the expression in his eyes as he studied her grandfather made her shiver.

These two men were sworn enemies—

'Clumsy—' Her grandfather shot her an impatient look and then turned to his host. 'Believe it or not, my granddaughter can walk when she applies her mind to the task. But like most women she's empty-headed.'

Alesia dipped her head rather than risk displaying the flash of anger that she knew must be visible in her eyes. Only by focusing on thoughts of her beloved mother did she prevent herself from stalking back to the helicopter and demanding return passage to the mainland.

She had to forget how much she hated her grandfather.

She had to forget how much she loathed the whole Fiorukis family.

She had to forget all of it.

The only thing that mattered was getting Sebastien Fiorukis to marry her.

No matter what happened, she would save her mother.

CHAPTER TWO

SHE was stunning.

Sebastien watched the silken blonde hair fall forward, obscuring her features, but not before he'd caught a glimpse of eyes the colour of violets in a perfect heart-shaped face. His gaze fixed on her smooth, creamy skin and then drifted down to her lush pink mouth. Her face alone was amazing, but combined with the body…

His eyes drifted lower. *Obvious*, he thought to himself scathingly, as he scanned the obscenely short dress that revealed tantalizingly long legs and fabulously generous breasts. Nothing was left to the imagination. Clearly the Philipos heiress had no reservations about displaying *exactly* what was on offer, he mused as his eyes settled on the temptingly full curves of her cleavage. But then she was selling herself for a ridiculously high price, he reminded himself cynically, so perhaps it was understandable that she felt he should be able to view the goods.

And view them he did.

Lust, basic and primitive, slammed through him, astonishing him by its very force. He was a man who had been fed a diet of beautiful women since he was a teenager and these days it took a lot to hold his attention.

But this girl was *definitely* holding his attention…

Suddenly the deal on the table before him took on new dimensions. Whatever Dimitrios Philipos had in mind, marrying his granddaughter could hardly be considered a hardship. Whatever else might be wrong with her, she certainly wasn't ugly and he *certainly* wouldn't have a problem being confined to bed with her on the occasions when it suited him.

Accustomed to being on the receiving end of non-stop female admiration and flirtation and confident of her response to him, Sebastien relaxed and waited for her to notice him in the way he'd *definitely* been noticing her.

It came as a considerable surprise to realize that she didn't seem remotely interested in his opinion of her attributes. Instead she stared at the ground, her chest rising and falling, her slim fingers digging hard into her palms, her knuckles white.

Scared?

Angry?

Sebastien attempted to read the body language and his speculative gaze slid to her grandfather, searching for answers. His body stilled as he caught the ugly expression on the older man's face. *The man was a bully and a thug.* And in this case the object of his aggression was undoubtedly the girl. Struggling with a base instinct that erupted from nowhere and surprised him with its intensity, Sebastien ruthlessly subdued the impulse to violently floor the man.

Was he forcing her into this marriage?

Experienced enough to know that women were complex creatures at the best of times, Sebastien decided to reserve judgement. He already knew that she'd inherited her grandfather's obscene thirst for wealth—why else would she be demanding such ridiculous sums from him on a monthly basis when she was already in possession of an indecent fortune?

And he couldn't even blame that aspect of the deal on her grandfather because she was to be the only recipient. Apparently her grandfather stood to gain nothing financially from a merger between their two families except a longed-for grandchild.

Torn between irritation with his father for creating this situation and fascination with the mind of his enemy, Sebastien tried to open a dialogue between them.

'Your journey was good, Miss Philipos?'

She displayed not a flicker of a response. It was as if she hadn't recognized her own name, he thought grimly, contemplating her complete lack of reaction with a deepening frown. Perhaps she preferred informality. 'Alesia?'

Immediately her eyes flew to his, astonishment lighting the blue depths, as if she were surprised that he was addressing her. 'Yes?'

Finally he had her attention. 'I asked whether your journey was good.' He dealt her a smile that never failed to gain female attention but she missed it because her gaze had returned to a point somewhere near his feet.

Sebastien hid his frustration. It was as if she couldn't bear to look at him. She was a complete contradiction. Her dress shrieked attention-seeking and yet her body language said something entirely different.

'It was fine, thank you.' She kept her eyes fixed firmly on the Tarmac and he noticed that her breathing was rapid, as if she was under immense strain.

Deciding that his first priority was to remove her from the presence of her grandfather, Sebastien took control. 'Walk with me while the lawyers argue the details. There are things we need to talk about.'

Immediately on the defensive, Dimitrios Philipos hunched his shoulders aggressively and stepped forward. 'She stays with me.'

Not budging an inch, Sebastien arched a dark eyebrow expressively. 'Is this proposed marriage to take place between three people or two?' His tone was dangerously soft. 'Are you intending to be present on our wedding night?'

He heard a soft gasp of shock from the girl standing by his side but ignored her, all his attention focused on the grandfather whose stance was now blatantly confrontational.

'If you knew my reputation you wouldn't choose to pick a fight with me, Fiorukis.'

Undeterred by his threatening tone, Sebastien gave a cool smile, ignoring his father's warning glance. 'I've never been afraid of a fight. And if you knew *my* reputation, you'd know that I choose to conduct my personal relationships in private. I've never been into groups.'

At that less than subtle reference to his own sordid reputation, Dimitrios Philipos glared at his rival for a long moment and then gave a grunt. 'Very well.' He gave a brief nod of assent, his expression grim. 'She might as well see her new home.'

Given that the deal was yet to be signed by either party, the statement was decidedly premature but Sebastien's natural instinct to deny such an assumption was stifled by a gasp of horror from the girl in question.

'My new home?' She glanced around her with naked alarm, suddenly roused from silence by her grandfather's statement. 'This would be our home? You'd want me to live *here*?'

Dragging his eyes from her slim legs, Sebastien gritted his teeth, barely able to hide his impatience.

Familiar with women who lived to shop, he rarely if ever brought his female companions to his island, accustomed to that very reaction from other members of her sex. It would seem that his prospective bride was no different. But, given the size of the financial deal her grandfather had negotiated on her behalf, that shouldn't have come as a surprise. What would a woman do with such an exorbitant sum if she didn't have access to a significant number of designer boutiques?

Sebastien narrowed his eyes, something about the whole situation jarring uncomfortably in his sharp brain.

His innate business sense warned him that this deal didn't feel quite right and he mentally shifted through different angles, seeking answers to the questions stacking up in his mind. And the main question was: *What did the Philipos heiress stand to gain from a union with a Fiorukis?*

Why would the granddaughter of the richest man on the planet need to marry him for money? Still pondering that question, Sebastien studied Dimitrios Philipos and caught the cold, avaricious gleam in the older man's eyes. Remembering his reputation for being the ultimate miser, Sebastien decided that he probably restricted her spending, which was why she was looking for other sources of income. He'd known loads of women who made a career out of marrying rich men. If granddaddy was no longer a soft touch then she'd need to look for some other sucker to pick up her bills. And, judging from her horrified reaction to the idea of being sequestered on an island without a boutique in sight, those bills were going to be *big*.

A flicker of contempt shot through him but he dismissed it with almost bored indifference. So she was greedy. He gave a mental shrug. That didn't come as a surprise.

Reminding himself that her motives had never been in question, he hid his distaste. 'I also have houses in Athens, Paris and New York,' he drawled lazily, 'so if you're concerned about the opportunity to exercise my credit card, then you can relax.'

Her eyes were fixed on the sea and she seemed not to have heard him.

Sebastien suppressed his irritation. Clearly he had been right in his assessment that she would have no personality. Even though he'd invariably thought that women generally talked *far* too much about very little of interest, he was finding the reverse considerably less satisfying than he would have imagined. Why on earth didn't the woman say something? Unaccustomed to such a lack of interest Sebastien decided that the sooner he got her on her own, the better.

'You don't like the island?' His tone was conversational and she shot him an agonized glance.

'There's lots of sea.'

That was most definitely *not* the answer he'd expected.

'There generally is when you live on an island. All the bedrooms in my villa open on to the beach or the pool.'

If he'd expected an enthusiastic response to that announcement then he was again disappointed. Instead of the delight he'd anticipated, her face seemed to pale dramatically.

Sebastien frowned. Was there something wrong with her?

'My granddaughter feels sick after the journey,' her grandfather grunted and Sebastien felt another surge of irritation with the older man.

Did he never let the girl speak for herself?

And surely if she'd been brought up in England she was used to expressing her own opinions?

Aware that the deal could not be concluded without his signature on the document, Sebastien focused on the girl. 'I will take Miss Philipos and show her the island while you two begin the meeting—I'll join you shortly.'

Dimitrios Philipos glanced at his watch. 'I have to be back in Athens in two hours. I want the deal signed before I leave.'

Sebastien watched him closely. The older man was definitely up to something. *Why the hurry?*

He was nothing like she'd expected.

Alesia stared in frozen silence at the man standing in front of her, her gaze resting on the width of his shoulders before lifting to his cool black eyes. Bold brows framed night-dark eyes and his strong nose accentuated the perfect symmetry of his staggeringly handsome face.

She'd been bred to hate this man.

In vain she searched for some evidence that he was as unsettled by this bizarre, awkward situation as she was but she found none. She sensed without even speaking to him that he was a man who would never find himself discomfited by any situation. Instead he studied her through narrowed eyes, the expression on his sinfully masculine face revealing nothing of his inner thoughts. He wore authority with the ease of a man who'd been born with a ferocious talent at business and had proceeded to exercise it at every opportunity.

Alesia looked at him helplessly.

How could this ever work out?

Ludicrously rich and breathtakingly good-looking, he was *totally*, totally out of her league and it was utterly mortifying to know that if her grandfather hadn't offered him a significant 'inducement' and dressed her in such a ridiculous dress he wouldn't have looked twice in her direction.

She felt like a total fraud.

Alesia bit back a burst of hysterical laughter. What would he do if he knew that she lived in a tiny damp flat? That she held down three jobs in an attempt to make ends meet? *That the dress she was wearing was the only one she had and even that was on loan?*

The thought of being alone with this man quite simply terrified her. What on earth would they talk about? What did they have in common?

Nothing.

And, to make matters worse, he clearly loved the sea.

Alesia kept her eyes fixed on the ocean and for a moment it all came rushing back. The sudden force of the explosion, the horrified screams of the injured and the sudden plunge into freezing water which buried her in a darkness so frightening that the memories still kept her awake at night. And then there were the memories of a man, dark-haired and strong, lifting her. Saving her—

Suddenly the price of saving her mother seemed almost too high.

She would have to live here, on an island, surrounded by sea that terrified her, living with a man she despised.

She gave herself a mental shake and dragged her gaze away from the water. She didn't have to swim or even to paddle, she reminded herself firmly. All she needed to do was remember the reason she was here. To play the part she'd schooled herself to play.

And she knew *exactly* why her grandfather had given the Fiorukis family a deadline of two hours to complete the deal. He was afraid that, left on her own with the man, she'd blow it. That she'd do something to put Sebastien Fiorukis off marrying her.

And he was right. She was so different from his usual choice of woman that the comparison was laughable. She couldn't even do a decent job of walking in the shoes.

'As far as I'm aware there is no language barrier between us,' he said smoothly, his dark gaze resting on her face with a significant degree of speculation, 'and yet so far you have uttered barely a word and cast barely a glance in my direction.'

Clearly she'd dented his monumental ego.

Alesia stifled a cynical laugh. *Was that all he cared about?* That she hadn't gazed into his eyes and fallen for him like the other brainless women he mixed with? He was *unbelievably* shallow and, as far as she was concerned, Sebastien Fiorukis deserved everything that was coming to him.

'You must forgive me—' her voice sounded stilted '—I—I'm finding this situation rather difficult—'

'Me, too. And that's hardly surprising given the circumstances. It's not every day you are expected to agree to a marriage to someone you have only just met. But this proposed marriage between us is going to be somewhat heavy weather if you can't bring yourself to speak to me,' he drawled lightly, and she met his gaze full-on.

'Am I supposed to speak honestly?'

'Why else did I just get rid of your grandfather?'

She almost smiled at the reminder of how neatly he'd dismissed her relative. Whatever else he might be, Sebastien Fiorukis was evidently *not* a coward. In fact he was the first person she'd met who didn't seem remotely intimidated by her grandfather, which was at least something in his favour. But nevertheless she was agonizingly aware that one wrong word from her could blow the whole deal.

'My grandfather is afraid that I'll say the wrong thing. He wants this deal very badly.'

'And you, Miss Philipos?' There was something dangerously soothing about his voice. Like a lethal predator stalking his prey. 'How badly do you want this deal?'

Being called 'Miss Philipos' felt totally alien. It was as if he was addressing a stranger. But it was all part of this act she was expected to maintain.

She lifted her chin. 'I want to marry you, if that's what you're asking.'

That at least was true. She *did* want to marry him. It would solve all her problems.

And all her mother's problems.

There was a sardonic gleam in his dark eyes as he watched her carefully. 'Don't tell me—' his voice was a deep, dark drawl '—you have been madly in love with me for your whole life? You have dreamed of this moment from your cradle, perhaps?'

She'd dreamed of having access to enough money to finally help her mother.

'I'm not in love with you, Mr Fiorukis, any more than you are in love with me,' she said calmly, 'and we both know that love is not the only reason for marriage.'

His spectacular eyes narrowed. 'Nevertheless, since we are the two people who will be forced to live together as a result of this deal, I think it's important to discover whether we can at least tolerate each other's company, don't you?' He gestured towards a narrow path that led down to the beach. 'Let's walk.'

She followed his gaze. The sea stretched into the distance like a cruel, forbidding monster, mocking her. The breath jammed in her throat and the panic rose.

'Can't we just stand here?'

'You wish to conduct a conversation on my helicopter pad?' His dark drawl dripped sarcasm and she flushed, still struggling as cold fingers of panic threatened to drag her down into darkness.

'I just don't see why we need to walk down to the sea.' This was close enough. *Too close.*

He glanced at her with barely concealed irritation. 'I refuse to conduct a conversation with your bodyguards hovering in the background.'

Her *bodyguards*?

Alesia glanced over her shoulder. She hadn't even *noticed* the three burly men until this moment, even though they must have been on the helicopter. She'd been too busy concentrating on not looking at the ocean. 'Oh—they work for my grandfather.'

'You don't need to explain. As the Philipos heiress you are entitled to protection.'

Momentarily forgetting her concerns about the sea and her shoes, Alesia almost laughed aloud. Protection from what? Who would be interested in a penniless, gawky student who spent every waking hour working herself to the bone? But clearly he knew nothing of her real life. Glancing around her, she noticed two other men hovering close by. 'Who are they?'

His smile mocked her. 'I'm afraid my own security team is naturally suspicious. Let's just say that a Philipos landing on the island creates a certain level of tension.'

She glanced briefly at his powerful shoulders and wondered why he needed a security team. He looked capable of taking on an entire army single-handed should the need arise. For a man who spent his days involved in business, he was supremely fit and athletic. Perhaps it was the hours he spent in bed with women, she mused idly, stepping to one side to avoid a dip in the path.

'My grandfather creates tension wherever he goes.' She spoke without thinking and then remembered too late who she was talking to and coloured. 'I mean to say—'

'Don't feel you have to excuse yourself to me,' he drawled softly. 'Grown men shiver in their shoes when your grandfather enters a room. It is part of the reputation he has built for himself. He manages by fear.'

But didn't Sebastien have the same reputation?

Wasn't she about to marry a man *exactly* like her grandfather?

Looking at the hovering bodyguards, she gave a shiver and made a decision. 'All right, let's walk on the beach.' She stooped to remove the shoes her grandfather had insisted she wear. 'Three-inch heels and sand don't go together.'

She saw the brief flash of astonishment in his beautiful dark eyes and realized her mistake immediately. Doubtless the women that he dated would be capable of climbing Everest in stilettos if the need arose.

'I like to feel the sand between my toes,' she improvised quickly, cursing her stupidity and making a mental note to take a crash course in suitable footwear as a matter of urgency.

'Be careful not to cut your feet on the rocks,' he said smoothly, reaching out a hand and taking hers in a strong grasp. Long fingers curled over hers and she felt an almost irresistible urge to drag her hand away. 'Those shoes are stunning and do amazing things for your legs. But on reflection I agree that they're probably better suited to a nightclub. I have several favourites so I can promise you that you'll have ample opportunity to wear them in a more suitable setting.'

Nightclubs?

Alesia glanced at him blankly, realising with no small degree of consternation that he clearly believed her to be a real party-girl. What would he say if she confessed that she'd never actually been to a nightclub in her life? That her demanding working pattern ensured that she rarely if ever had an evening off to enjoy such indulgences?

Quickly she steered the conversation away from such dangerous subjects. 'So, if you don't trust my grandfather, why did you invite him to your island—?'

They had negotiated the rock successfully and yet strong fingers still held her securely. 'This deal is important to me for many reasons.' He glanced at her thoughtfully. 'You are surely not pretending to know nothing about the feud that exists between our families?'

Her breathing quickened and she snatched her hand away. 'Of course I'm aware of the feud—'

My father was killed on your father's boat; my mother and I were both injured.

Emotion rose inside her until she could hardly breathe. *Until it threatened to choke her.* She felt him watching her and struggled for control.

Alesia turned away in distaste, still clutching her shoes in her hand. Only the most rigid self-discipline allowed her to continue the conversation with this man.

'I think before we go any further you should know that, despite the fact that my grandfather would want me to, I don't play games. I can't pretend something I don't feel,' she said coldly. 'I don't flirt and I refuse to pretend that this marriage is anything other than a business arrangement between two parties. We each get something we want.'

'And what exactly is that, Miss Philipos?'

'Money,' she said succinctly, lifting her chin and looking him in the eye. 'I get money.'

'Straight to the point. You are the only living relative of the richest man on the planet and yet still you want more,' Sebastien drawled, his gaze suddenly speculative, 'which probably makes you the biggest gold-digger in history. Tell me, Alesia—' he said her name with mocking emphasis '—just how much money is enough?'

By now they were standing on a stretch of perfect golden sand. Alesia concentrated on the man next to her, keeping her back to the azure-blue sea which sparkled and shone in the intense heat of the Greek summer sun. To her it represented nothing but terror.

'Given your own wealth, I could ask you the same question. You already have a company that nets you billions and still you want what belongs to my grandfather.'

'That's right, I do.' His smile was sardonic. 'But I'm not going to *quite* the lengths that you are to achieve that goal. For money you are prepared to tie yourself to your greatest enemy. A man that you clearly hate—'

A sudden attack of panic assailed her. She'd revealed too much. *He mustn't back out of the deal.* 'I didn't say that—'

'You didn't need to,' he said drily. 'It is apparent from every flash of your eyes, from the way you hold yourself and from all the things that you *don't* say, that you hate me with every bone in your body.'

Alesia could barely breathe as she cursed her stupidity.

Her grandfather had warned her that the man was clever and she'd ignored him. Had dismissed everything he'd said as yet another part of his plan. But in this case he was right. Sebastien Fiorukis *was* clever.

He was clever, dangerous and every bit a match for her grandfather.

'I don't hate you,' she lied hastily and he lifted a winged brow.

'I should warn you that I am a man who prefers honesty,' he said softly, 'even when it is distasteful. You've just admitted that you're prepared to marry a man that you hate for money. Now, what sort of person does that make you, I wonder?'

She almost choked with outrage. He made her sound

dreadful. If only he knew why she wanted the money, he might not be so swift to judge her.

She stared him in the eye. 'Let's just say that I'm more than satisfied with the financial arrangements that are to be a part of this contract.'

The accusation was so false, *so far from reality*, that for a wild, uncontrolled moment she almost blurted out the truth. But to confess the truth would be to blow the whole deal. And she needed this deal for her mother. What did it matter what he thought of her? What did it matter if he thought she was a money-grabbing gold-digger? If he discovered her grandfather's shoddy treatment of both her and her mother then he would *never* believe that her grandfather wanted this deal for her benefit. He'd realize that her grandfather was so far from being the 'family man' that he was pretending to be that something more sinister was afoot.

He'd sense that her grandfather was after revenge.

'Well, you're prepared to marry the granddaughter of your greatest enemy just to get his company. And you already have your own company that makes you *billions*. So what sort of a person does that make *you*?'

'Rich enough to afford you,' he responded in cool tones, his eyes hard as they scanned her pale face. 'Your opinion of me is as low as mine is of you, which should make us extremely well-matched. It will be a pleasant change not to have to charm a woman when I come home tired from a day in the office. I think marriage may suit me after all.'

'You wouldn't be able to charm me if you tried,' she said stiffly, made *furious* by his overwhelming arrogance. 'And, just for the record, I'm not remotely interested in experiencing your *superior* bedroom technique. That isn't what this marriage is about.'

'Is that so?' He smiled and stepped closer to her and suddenly she was aware of nothing but heat and she wondered how on *earth* she was going to be able to stand living in

Greece. The atmosphere was so still and oppressive that she could barely draw breath. Her skin tingled and buzzed and she felt *strange*.

'This is a business arrangement,' she reminded him coldly, and his dark eyes gleamed.

'A business arrangement—' He repeated her words thoughtfully, his eyes fixed on her face as he studied her every reaction. 'Tell me—do you know how babies are made, Miss Philipos?'

The temperature of the air surrounding her seemed to increase dramatically.

Colour flared in her cheeks and her toes dug into the sand. 'What sort of a question is that?'

'A sensible one,' he replied smoothly, 'given that the production of a baby is generally preceded by sexual activity, with or without *"superior bedroom technique"*. Tell me, does your "business arrangement" include sexual activity, Miss Philipos?'

Totally shocked by the lethal intimacy of his tone and the sudden shift in the focus of the discussion, her eyes widened and she gave a soft gasp.

'I—I don't—'

'No?' His tone hardened and his gaze was unsympathetic. 'And yet that is what this deal is all about. Tell me, Miss Philipos, just how exactly do you envisage this "business arrangement" taking place? Do you intend to bring your briefcase to my bed?'

She inhaled sharply as all sorts of uncomfortably blatant images assailed her brain.

Somehow she'd managed to convince herself that this whole thing could be a relatively straightforward arrangement. He could live his life. She could live hers. The issue of a sexual relationship had crossed her mind briefly, of course, but somehow the notion of sex with a man she'd never met had seemed abstract. Unreal.

But face to face there was nothing unreal about Sebastien Fiorukis. He was six foot two of full-on, sexual, adult male.

Suddenly the sex aspect of their agreement didn't seem quite so straightforward as she'd previously imagined it to be.

For a moment she forgot about the sea and her grandfather and focused on the appalling reality of sliding between the sheets with this hot-blooded volatile Greek.

'Not a briefcase.' Struggling to pull herself together, she answered his sardonic question as calmly as she could, ignoring the kick of her heart and the strange buzz in the pit of her stomach. 'But clearly there will be no emotional involvement between us. I will have sex with you because that is what the contract demands, but nowhere does it say that I am required to enjoy the experience.' She caught his incredulous gaze. 'And that's fine,' she added hastily, suddenly extremely anxious to reassure him that her enjoyment was *not* on his list of objectives.

'You'll "have sex" with me?' Sebastien stared at her in fascination, night-black eyes raking her face as he repeated her words.

Alesia closed her eyes. The problem was, he was used to women who expected to be seduced. She didn't. In fact she couldn't think of anything worse. She wasn't remotely interested in sex and never had been. Once she'd discovered that she'd never be able to have children, she'd buried that part of herself away. And it no longer mattered to her. The few kisses she'd experienced since reaching adolescence had proved to her that she just wasn't interested.

Realising that the situation was rapidly sliding out of control, she gave a frustrated sigh and tried one more time to make him see logic. 'Look—this isn't about you.' She tried clumsily to rescue his ego from any damage inflicted by her remark. 'This isn't personal. We just won't have that sort of marriage. And that's fine. I mean really—' she spread her hands in a nervous gesture, wondering how on earth this conversation had begun '—it's how I want it.'

He stirred, his gaze still fixed on her face. 'Clearly you have always had lousy sex.'

Hot colour flooded her cheeks and she looked away quickly, trying to regain some semblance of control.

Perhaps this was the point where she was supposed to tell him that she'd *never* had sex before but there was no way she was doing that! It was too embarrassing to have reached the grand old age of twenty-two and still be a virgin and she was totally confident that when the time came she could successfully hide her massive lack of experience in that department.

'So you're prepared to marry me and have "businesslike sex"—' his tone was dangerously casual '—and I pay you for the privilege. Interesting concept and one that I confess I'm unfamiliar with. I've never before found myself in a position where I had to pay for sex.'

'Of course you have.' She responded without thinking. 'Women hang round you hoping that you'll spend your billions on them and in return they fawn over you and pretend to find you attractive—if that's not paying for sex, I don't know what is. And in this case you're not paying for sex, you're paying for my grandfather's company.'

He looked totally stunned by this less than flattering interpretation of his love life and Alesia struggled not to roll her eyes in exasperation. His ego was positively monumental! He obviously thought that women wanted to be with him because he was completely irresistible. He was *so* sad!

'You're a rich man, Sebastien,' she said impatiently, using his given name as he had used hers. 'You can't be telling me that I'm the first woman to be interested in your money.'

His dark eyes narrowed and he finally found his voice. 'Let's just say that you're the first *seriously rich* woman to be interested in my money. Why would you need it so much, I wonder?'

If only he knew.

Alesia dangled the shoes under his nose, her gaze intentionally provocative. 'Perhaps I just have *enormous* spending powers.'

She almost laughed as she listened to herself. The truth was that she wouldn't have a clue how to spend money if she had it. Apart from her time at boarding school, she'd lived in virtual poverty for her entire life and economizing came as naturally to her as breathing. If she *was* pointed in the direction of a designer boutique, she'd probably just drop to her knees and start scrubbing the floor.

The dress she was wearing was the first new item of clothing she'd had for as long as she could remember and she only had that because her grandfather had taken one look at her ancient pair of faded jeans and almost burst a blood vessel. When she'd pointed out tartly that she didn't have the money for a dress, he'd barked out a series of orders to one of his staff and three dresses had duly been chosen. But even then she hadn't been given the option of selecting her favourite. Instead she'd been subjected to the humiliation of modelling all three in front of her grandfather, and had the added humiliation of being forced to wear the most revealing garment she'd ever laid eyes on.

'You need to show the man what he's getting,' he'd grunted when she'd protested that there was no way she could wear a dress that was that low-cut. 'Wear it or the deal is off.'

So she'd forced herself into the offending garment and tried not to show how utterly self-conscious she was to be wearing such a totally unsuitable dress. As far as she was concerned, the dress said one thing, *'Pull me',* and she had the sense to realize that, given her appearance, mentioning her virginity to Sebastien Fiorukis at this point would do nothing but engender laughter.

'I can see that my honesty offends you,' she said smoothly, lifting her chin to hide her discomfort, 'but perhaps I can remind you that you yourself are entering this marriage for sound business reasons. Why else would you agree to sacrifice your bachelor lifestyle for marriage?'

'Who said anything about sacrificing my bachelor lifestyle?' His firm mouth shifted slightly at the corners. 'It's only fair to warn you that I have an *exceedingly* high sex drive. Since our sex life is clearly going to be extremely tedious, then I'll need to seek diversion elsewhere. But I'm prepared to pay that price in order to regain possession of Philipos Industries. The company that your grandfather stole from my family.'

She frowned. 'I don't know what you're talking about. Philipos Industries belongs to my grandfather and always has.'

'Not true.' His gaze was hard. 'And if you expect me to believe that you don't know the history of our little family feud, Miss Philipos, then you seriously underestimate me. You wanted honesty, then let's have it.'

She swallowed hard. She didn't underestimate him. Not for a moment. She was just thrown by his unexpected announcement. 'Are you telling me that our grandparents were in business together?'

His eyes narrowed. 'Are you telling me that you weren't aware of that fact?'

She shook her head. 'My grandfather refuses to discuss business with a woman.' At least that wasn't a lie, she thought ruefully. Her grandfather despised women. Especially English women. It was the reason he'd disowned her mother and herself. He'd wanted nothing to do with either of them. 'I've heard rumours, of course, but nothing concrete.

Are you saying that he took the business from your grand-father?'

'It is how the feud began.' Sebastien looked at her, his dark gaze suddenly speculative. 'He lied and cheated until my grandfather was forced to sign the company over to him,' he bit out, his expression grim. 'So you see, Alesia, I want to marry you because I intend to reclaim what is rightfully mine. And the feud ends here.'

Alesia stared at him, for once totally mute.

What would he say when he discovered the truth? That the feud hadn't ended at all.

That her grandfather was about to strike a master blow.

And she was the tool of his revenge.

CHAPTER THREE

PALE-FACED and utterly miserable, Alesia sat shivering in her white silk wedding dress, feeling *nothing* like a bride.

Despite the gold band on her finger, part of her still couldn't believe that she'd actually gone through with the wedding.

Oblivious to the elaborate celebrations taking place around her, she stared blankly at her plate and tried to focus her mind.

She'd actually married Sebastien Fiorukis.

It seemed hard to believe that only two weeks had passed since their meeting on his private island. Since then everything had been a blur of frantic activity. Lawyers had worked overtime, papers had been signed and wedding planners had burned the midnight oil to put together the wedding of the decade.

To Alesia the ceremony had been a nightmare.

Why hadn't she anticipated the attention that such a high-profile wedding would attract? For the press, who were eternally fascinated by Sebastien Fiorukis, the fact that he'd finally chosen to marry the granddaughter of his greatest enemy had sent an explosion of excitement and speculation through the gossip-hungry media. Knowing that personal details of the handsome Greek billionaire sold newspapers, the press had been everywhere, flashes going off in her face and people yelling at her to smile and glance in their direction.

And of course the wedding attracted even more attention because of the presence of her notorious grandfather. Dimitrios Philipos so rarely appeared in public that his presence alone was enough to draw a crowd of fascinated onlookers. Everyone wanted to witness a public meeting between Fiorukis and Philipos. Everyone was anticipating fireworks.

Sebastien had handled the attention and simmering speculation with an air of almost bored disdain, ignoring reporters, greeting guests with just the right amount of attention and interest, as comfortable and confident as he'd been during that first awful meeting.

In contrast, Alesia had taken one horrified look at the jostling, over-excited paparazzi and kept her eyes firmly fixed on the ground in an attempt to blot out what was happening.

She didn't want people to be interested in her.

She knew that journalists had a way of digging up secrets. *What if they dug up hers?*

What if something happened to stop the wedding? To prevent her mother from having the operation she so badly needed?

Terrified that someone would say something to halt the ceremony, she'd stood at the front of the church like a frightened rabbit, hardly daring to breathe in case she drew attention to herself, *in case someone recognized her for the impostor that she was.*

She'd worn the long white wedding dress that her grandfather had presented her with, pulled the veil over her face and hoped that none of the guests would notice her wan face or the fact that she was *seriously* out of her depth. Playing the role of rich heiress was totally new to her.

When she realized that they were safely married the relief had been so great that she'd almost passed out.

Once or twice it had crossed her mind that this wasn't the way weddings were supposed to be, that this was supposed to be a happy day. But then she reminded herself firmly that she'd never been one to dream and fantasize about weddings, so it wasn't possible for her to be disappointed that hers hadn't lived up to expectation. She didn't have any expectation.

'You could try and look a little more like an excited bride and less like someone being led to torture,' Sebastien suggested silkily, snapping his fingers at the waiter and indicating that he should top up their glasses. 'This is, after all, what you wanted. You've landed yourself a billionaire. Smile.'

Alesia grabbed the glass gratefully and drank deeply, her loathing for Sebastien Fiorukis increasing by the minute. He was cold, unfeeling and just *horrid*. At least she was thoroughly uncomfortable with the situation but he just didn't seem to care that they didn't even like each other.

All right, so she *was* marrying him for the money, she conceded, but that was completely different because she was *desperate*. Unlike him. He was already a billionaire. He already had one company. Only someone who was impossibly greedy could want *two*!

Alesia shivered as she contemplated the man she'd married.

He was just like her grandfather. Rich, successful, restless and never satisfied.

Maybe champagne would help. She didn't normally drink but wasn't alcohol supposed to numb the senses? She sincerely hoped so. The way she was feeling, she needed her senses rendered unconscious. Returning the empty glass to the table, she sucked several breaths into her lungs and tried hard to forget that everyone was watching her. Speculating. Why hadn't someone warned her that Sebastien had such a large family? And so many friends—

'I wasn't expecting all this—'

'It's called a wedding,' Sebastien said helpfully, smiling briefly at a stunning woman who cast a longing glance towards him as she slid past on the arm of a male guest, 'and it's what you signed up for when you agreed to marry me for my money. Enjoy it. It's costing enough. Look on it as retail therapy.'

Money.

Grateful for the reminder, Alesia took another slug of champagne and forced herself to focus. All she had to do was remember the money. The reason she was doing this. It didn't matter that everyone was staring at her. It didn't matter that everyone was wondering why Sebastien Fiorukis had chosen to marry her. *It didn't matter that she felt lonelier than she had in her whole life.* All that mattered was that at last—*finally*—her beloved mother would get the treatment she needed so badly.

She glanced sideways at the man sitting next to her. *The man she'd married.* He lounged beside her, totally relaxed and well within his comfort zone, as if marrying a total stranger was something he did every day of his life. Outwardly he was the type of man women the world round drooled over. Sophisticated, spoiled and so ridiculously wealthy that he could never have understood in a million years how it felt to be poor. How it felt to be so desperate for money that you'd do *anything*—even marry a man you'd been raised to hate.

His suit was dark and accentuated every inch of masculine perfection. His shoulders were wide, his frame powerful and athletic and he wore his looks with the ease and assurance of a man who'd been born with the entire silver cutlery set in his mouth.

He'd never known poverty and he'd never known hardship.

How could he ever understand what had driven her to this moment? A flash of panic suddenly assailed her. What if he backed out of their agreement? The man was every bit as ruthless and money-mad as her grandfather. She'd been naïve and stupid to trust him. She should have checked. She should have rung the bank—

She turned to him, her heart pounding uncomfortably in her chest as she contemplated the various scenarios, all of them awful.

'Has the money been transferred to my account?' The question flew from her lips unbidden and she immediately clamped her mouth shut and wished it unsaid as spectacular dark eyes fixed on hers with unconcealed disdain.

'Even as we speak,' he drawled softly, his firm mouth tightening into a grim line. 'I'm surprised you're not begging to miss the reception so that you can go and spend, spend, spend.'

Feeling relief wash over her she relaxed slightly, telling herself that his opinion of her really didn't matter. All that mattered was her mother. And anyway, Sebastien Fiorukis was hardly in a position to criticize her for wanting money. She glanced down at the gold watch that nestled in the dark hairs of his wrist. The watch alone was probably worth more than she spent in a year.

'And my grandfather's company?'

'Now belongs to me,' he said dryly, reaching for his glass, 'along with a substantial quantity of debts and enough labour-relation problems to ensure that my time is fully occupied for the foreseeable future. I'm afraid it's going to delay our honeymoon, *pethi mou*.'

Honeymoon?

Her eyes flew to his, startled. She hadn't thought any further than the wedding day. She certainly hadn't contemplated the fact that he might be planning a honeymoon. Panic knotted deep in her stomach. 'I—I didn't think we'd be having a honeymoon—'

'Honeymoons are for lovers,' he slotted in with a grim smile, 'which is what we are supposed to be. But at the moment I haven't got time for a wife. So there's no honeymoon.'

Alesia closed her eyes briefly and breathed a sigh of relief.

A honeymoon would have been unbearable. As it was, hope-fully he'd be too busy to spend any time with her. They could lead separate lives.

Alesia sucked in a breath and forced herself to relax. It would be fine, she assured herself. They barely needed to see each other. This was her life now. She really had to try and adapt.

Her eyes scanned the enormous garden that was the setting for the reception, taking in the glitz and the glamour. Guests had flown in from all over the globe to witness the wedding of Sebastien Fiorukis and everywhere she looked there were elegant women and rich, confident men.

Alesia bit her lip and dug her short, unmanicured nails into her palms.

Could they see through her? Did they realize that, despite being the 'Philipos heiress', she didn't move in these circles and never had? What would they say if they knew that nor-mally she dressed in jeans and waited on tables to earn extra money? What would they say if they knew she didn't have a penny to her name?

Except that now, she reminded herself as she lifted her glass to her lips, she *did* have a penny to her name. Thanks to her new husband, she was now an extremely wealthy woman. On paper. In reality the money was already spent. She'd set up an agreement with the bank so that the money was automatically transferred into her mother's medical fund.

'What are you planning, I wonder,' Sebastien purred, sur-veying her with a dangerous glint in his eyes. 'You look alarmingly like a woman who is plotting.'

Her eyes widened in alarm. 'I—I'm not plotting—'

'No? Then you'll be the first member of your sex who isn't.'

Before she could think of a suitable reply, he lifted a hand to her head and removed the elaborate clip with a decisive movement.

She gave a gasp of surprise and protest as her blonde hair unwound itself, slid down and settled over her shoulders. 'What are you doing?'

'I paid for you,' he said succinctly, his eyes fastened to her hair with undisguised masculine interest, 'and you were *very* expensive, *agape mou*. I therefore have the right to use you in any way I see fit.'

Alesia almost choked with outrage. 'You don't own me—'

'Oh, yes, I do.' He leaned towards her. 'I do own you, Alesia. Every single delectable part of you. I own your long silky hair and those amazing eyes that can almost convince me you're innocent even though I know you're a conniving, greedy little gold-digger. I own that fabulous body which you've doubtless used on countless occasions to persuade men to part with their money. I own the lot, Alesia. The deal we both signed was nothing short of a purchase on my part.'

She closed her eyes. 'You make me feel like a—like a—'

'Whore? Prostitute?' he supplied helpfully. 'I can see that the distinction might be difficult to make but you're obviously perfectly satisfied with your career choice and who can blame you? There are far worse ways of earning a substantial sum of money.'

She gave a gasp of outrage and her eyes flew open. 'Whatever you may think of me, I'm *not* promiscuous!'

'At the price that you charge, that is hardly surprising,' he drawled, a sardonic gleam in his dark eyes as they swept over her flushed cheeks. 'Clearly you know how to keep yourself exclusive. Only the richest can afford you.'

Deeply offended, her eyes flashed her distaste. 'I *hate* you,' she said passionately and he smiled.

'Maybe. But you need my money, *pethi mou*, which says a lot about your character, don't you agree?'

Overwhelmed by a sudden impulse to tell him exactly why

she needed the money, Alesia stared helplessly into his arrogant, handsome face and fought the impulse to slap it.

She couldn't tell him.

She'd come this far—

And she didn't need to defend herself to a man she didn't like or respect.

She rose to her feet, determined to put distance between them, but lean brown fingers closed around her slender wrist.

'If you're about to make an exhibition of yourself then think again,' he advised silkily, the expression in his eyes like a building thunderstorm. 'You're now my wife and I expect you to behave as such. This is not the time or the place for female tantrums. Everyone is looking at you. Sit down.'

Alesia tried to jerk her hand away but his grip tightened mercilessly and she sank back into her chair wondering how on earth she was going to get through the next hour with this man, let alone a lifetime.

Awash with hatred for him, she glanced up and saw a sultry-looking brunette staring at her with a stricken expression on her lovely face.

Alesia frowned. 'Now I see what you meant about people staring. She looks pretty upset,' she muttered, glancing sideways at Sebastien who was lounging in the chair next to her. 'Am I to assume she wanted to be sitting where I am?'

Part of her found it hard to believe that anyone would *choose* to marry Sebastien Fiorukis but there was no missing the misery in the other woman's gaze.

Sebastien fastened night-black eyes on the girl in question and gave the ghost of a smile. 'Quite a few women wanted to be sitting where you are, *pethi mou*,' he drawled, 'so you should just count yourself lucky.'

Lucky?

'Don't you even care that she's upset?' Alesia made a

sound of disgust. 'You are *totally* unfeeling. Perhaps she was in love with you. She might be heartbroken.'

'Heartbroken.' He studied her, his gaze speculative. 'Funny—I never would have thought you were a romantic. After all, you're the woman who just married for yet more money. Are you telling me you believe in love?'

Alesia bit her lip. 'She's *obviously* upset—'

He gave a cynical smile. 'So would you be if you saw your glamorous lifestyle threatened. Relax. Her affection is no more than wallet-deep. Her wounds will be healed by the next rich man foolish enough to glance in her direction.'

Alesia stared at him in appalled disbelief. 'Who have you spent your life mixing with? Where did you get *such* a low opinion of women?'

'From people like you, perhaps?' His tone was lethally smooth and she flushed deeply, knowing that she was in no position to contradict him.

How could she? She *did* want his money, even though it wasn't for her benefit.

'Let's not pretend that either of us believes in fairy tales or love.' His eyes fastened on hers. 'You certainly don't or you wouldn't be sitting here now.'

Love.

Glancing at the girl one more time, Alesia saw raw jealousy in her eyes and almost laughed at the irony of the situation.

Whatever the emotion driving her, the girl clearly wanted to be sitting where she was sitting. She was probably the envy of at least half the women in the world.

And she'd never felt more miserable in her life.

Alesia returned her gaze to her plate and almost jumped as she felt Sebastien cover her hand with his own.

Startled by his unexpected touch, she lifted her gaze to his and was instantly mesmerized by the look in his seductive dark eyes. It was a look that teased and tantalized, a promise of things to come, and for a moment she just stared, held captive by the sheer sexuality of his presence.

He had something that she'd never encountered before—

A magnetism. A—

He leaned towards her and she stopped breathing, waiting for him to speak. Waiting to hear what he suddenly wanted to say to her—

'My mother is about to come and speak to you,' Sebastien murmured softly in her ear, lean, bronzed fingers toying idly with a strand of her hair, 'and you are to say nothing which upsets her in any way, do I make myself clear? As far as she is concerned, we are crazy about each other. One wrong move on your part and the money stops.'

Crazy about each other?

Her heart thudding uncomfortably, Alesia froze. She was totally thrown by the contrast between the seduction in his eyes and the lethal tone of his voice.

There was no missing the warning in his tone.

'Surely she knows this is a business arrangement—' Her own voice was little more than a croak and she struggled to breathe. 'We only met two weeks ago.'

'My mother is a romantic,' he murmured, smiling down at her with what must have seemed to a casual observer a flattering degree of attentiveness. 'She believes that we were destined to meet and fall in love. The feud has come full circle. Your parents died and now we are together.'

Finding that she just couldn't think straight when he was leaning so close to her, Alesia swallowed hard and then turned to greet the woman who had approached while they'd been talking. They'd been introduced briefly before the ceremony but that was all and Alesia had barely paid attention. As far as she was concerned his mother was just another Fiorukis. Another member of the family who had been directly responsible for her father's death. She ought to hate her. She was the enemy.

Alesia stared up at Diandra Fiorukis, saw the warmth in her eyes and the pride in her expression and suddenly found she couldn't hate her. Nor could she see her as the enemy. She was just someone's mother.

A mother attending her beloved son's wedding. Proud. Nervous.

Drawn. *Strained.*

'You look beautiful, Alesia,' the older woman said wistfully. 'Your own mother would have been so proud of you if she could see you now.'

The reminder that her own mother didn't even know she was getting married tore at Alesia's heart. Her mother would have been *horrified* had she known that she was getting married. And to whom.

Unable to speak for a moment, knowing she couldn't reveal that her mother was alive, she struggled with the emotion that threatened to erupt inside her.

'This is a happy day for our two families. I'm pleased that your grandfather agreed to come today.' His mother settled herself in the chair next to her. 'Everyone wants family around them when they marry.'

Family?

Alesia remembered that his mother had no idea that she and her grandfather had only met two weeks earlier. That they had no relationship at all and never would.

That her grandfather had brutally cut both her mother and herself out of his life.

It was on the tip of her tongue to protest that she didn't consider her grandfather to be family, but fortunately she realized in time that such a statement would reveal far too much about the true situation and she couldn't risk that. There was still too much at stake. If they discovered that her mother was alive and that her grandfather had disowned both of them then they would guess that this wedding was about revenge, not unity.

Feeling guilty for deceiving the other woman, she changed the subject.

'I never realized Sebastien was part of such a large family,' she said stiffly, watching as yet another giggling teenager fought for his attention. Everywhere she turned there seemed to be sisters, cousins and aunts hugging him, small children waiting to crawl on to his lap.

His mother smiled serenely. 'They are your family too now.' She reached out and took Alesia's hand in hers. 'You've no idea how much I've longed for this moment. I thought Sebastien would never be willing to sacrifice his bachelor life for a girl. I'd given up hoping that he'd ever find anyone good enough for him.'

Seeing that the woman was genuinely moved, Alesia squirmed uncomfortably. She couldn't pretend—she just couldn't.

'My mother is a romantic,' Sebastien drawled, turning his attention from the younger members of his family to the older. 'She dreams only of happy endings.'

There was a clear warning in his eyes and Alesia clamped her lips together, holding back the words that she wanted to speak, reminding herself that she didn't have to apologise to these people. That she didn't have to explain herself.

'I dream of grandchildren,' his mother confessed, her eyes sparkling as she looked at Alesia. 'As I'm sure your grandfather does.'

Appalled by his mother's innocent expectations, Alesia felt a sick feeling build in the pit of her stomach.

Grandchildren.

And that, of course, was the one thing she was never going to be able to provide. She closed her eyes and told herself firmly that it didn't bother her what the Fiorukis family wanted. She *hated* them. She hated her grandfather and she hated their stupid feud. In fact she hated everything Greek because it embodied everything that had ruined her mother's life.

So why was she suddenly struck by conscience?

Sebastien lounged in his seat, watching his new bride through veiled eyes.

He considered himself something of an expert on the avarice of women, but even he was astonished by her almost indecent desire to get her hands on his money.

He was used to women who at least pretended to be interested in something other than his wallet but Alesia, it seemed, couldn't even be bothered to pretend. It was the *only* question she'd asked him. The only piece of information it seemed she needed of him. *'Has the money been transferred to my account?'*

Her total desperation shone through. All through the ceremony she'd been pale and anxious, her agitation so palpable that he'd started to wonder whether something was seriously the matter with his bride.

Anyone looking at her would think she *needed* the money.

He gave a grim smile, knowing full well that 'need' was a relative term and to the Philipos heiress need clearly encompassed greed of a magnitude that even he had failed to encounter in the past.

Aware that his mother was still watching them, he tried to find a mutually satisfying topic of conversation and drew a blank. 'So tell me,' he breathed sarcastically, relieved that his mother was not skilled in lip-reading, 'what will be your first purchase with your newfound wealth? A thousand pairs of designer shoes or something bigger? A yacht, maybe? A racehorse or two?'

She lifted her eyes from the contemplation of her untouched plate of food and stared at him blankly. 'Pardon?'

He frowned down at her, noticing for the first time the dark smudges under her eyes. Clearly she hadn't slept for nights. Probably worrying that the deal would fall through, he mused.

'I was asking how you plan to spend my money,' he repeated, realizing with a flash of surprise that she was paying him not the slightest bit of attention. He almost smiled at the irony of the situation. He was accustomed to employing a variety of skills designed to keep women at a distance and yet the woman he'd just married was having trouble remembering that he existed. 'I think I should at least know something about my wife.'

'Oh.' She frowned as if she were thrown by the question. There was a brief hesitation and something close to panic flashed in her eyes. 'I—I don't know yet—I expect I'll go—shopping?'

Sebastien refrained from pointing out that she truly would have to shop until she dropped if she stood even the faintest chance of spending even a fraction of the money he'd just delivered into her account.

Clearly he wouldn't be seeing much of his new wife, he mused grimly. To spend that volume of money was going to take a considerable length of time and serious application on her part.

Consumed by an irritation that he didn't begin to understand, he rose to his feet and extended a hand. 'Time to earn that money. We're expected to begin the dancing.'

She stared at him stupidly. 'Dance? You and I—together?'

He ground his teeth. 'It's tradition for man and wife to dance.' Without giving her time to argue, he hauled her against him and flashed a smile into her shocked face. 'Time to give the crowd what they've been waiting for, *pethi mou*.'

He strode purposefully on to the dance floor, his arm round her waist in what must have seemed to the wedding guests an affectionate gesture. In fact he was keeping her from running because he knew for a fact that if he released her she would *definitely* run.

She was staring up at him as if he'd gone completely mad. And perhaps he had, he reflected. After all, he had just married a woman whose values he despised. Hardly the action of a sane man.

'Smile up at me as if I'm the only man in the world,' he ordered softly as he stopped in the middle of the dance floor and curved an arm round her waist. 'We are the focus of attention and I would hate to disappoint our guests.'

'This is ridiculous.' Sebastien felt her stiffen, saw her teeth clench. 'I thought we agreed that we weren't going to play games. That we were going to be honest with each other.'

'In private, yes.' He lowered his face closer to hers so that there was no chance of being overheard. 'But to the outside world we have to create the right impression. My mother needs to think this marriage is real, the financial markets need to think this marriage is real. So we're going to make them think it's real.'

His attention was suddenly caught by her perfectly shaped mouth and for a moment he couldn't quite remember what was so important about the financial markets. Mesmerized by the soft curve of her lips, Sebastien watched as they parted slightly and a delicate pink tongue darted out nervously.

His whole body tightened in a primitive male response to the gesture of vulnerability.

'You're deluding yourself,' Alesia said shakily, her eyes darkening in consternation. 'No one looking at us can possibly think this marriage is anything other than a business arrangement.'

Reminding himself that there was nothing vulnerable about a wealthy woman who'd just married someone she clearly loathed, he dragged his eyes from her mouth.

'Then it's up to us to prove them wrong.' Without thinking, he pulled her hard against him in a gesture of pure possession and felt her quiver of shock as her body came into contact with his for the first time.

Awareness exploded between them and Sebastien stopped breathing. Shocked into stillness by the unexpected power of their mutual response. It was as if their bodies had recognized something that both of them had failed to notice. Alesia's subtle scent oozed over his senses and seduced his mind and body into forgetting everything except the woman in his arms.

Neither of them spoke but he saw her breathing go shallow, watched the pupils dilate in those amazing violet eyes as she acknowledged the throbbing tension in the atmosphere.

He felt her tremble against him and frowned slightly, registering for the first time just how delicate she was. She'd revealed enough of her full cleavage during that first meeting with her grandfather for him to have formed an impression that she was generously built, but now he realized how totally wrong he'd been in that initial assessment. With predictable masculine focus, he'd been seriously distracted. The rest of her was impossibly slender. *Fragile.*

Still shocked by the power of his response to her, Sebastien curved a hand over the base of her spine in brooding contemplation and gave a wry smile as he acknowledged the eternal weakness of man. His libido was clearly indifferent to the fact that she was a self-confessed gold-digger. But then what was wrong with that? Gold-digger or not, she was *incredibly* beautiful and he should be rejoicing that his new bride might well prove to have her compensations. Providing they didn't have to indulge in conversation, the forthcoming night promised to be *far* from boring.

Since he'd removed her hairclip, her blonde tresses poured down her back in a shiny silken sheet and he found himself resisting the temptation to bury his face in its scented mass.

She tried to pull away but he held her firmly, his gaze faintly mocking as he looked down at her.

'Amazing is it not,' he murmured softly, curving her

against him as they swayed in time to the music, 'that our bodies can feel something that our minds tell us not to?'

She planted a hand in the centre of his chest, panic in her eyes as she tried to hold him at a distance. 'I don't know what you're talking about.'

He removed her hand in a deliberate movement, pulled her closer still and lowered his head so that his mouth was only inches from hers. Her unexpectedly seductive scent made his head swim. 'Oh, yes, you do, you know *exactly* what I'm talking about.'

'What are you doing? Everyone is staring—'

So was he. He'd never seen eyes such an unusual shade of blue, he mused, his gaze still fixed on her face. The colour of English violets.

'For a self-confessed gold-digger you are extraordinarily sensitive,' he murmured in her ear, sliding his other arm round her and pulling her closer still. 'Why would you care what people think?'

'I just don't like being stared at.'

He gave a short laugh. She was an heiress, albeit a ridiculously protected one. 'Then you'd better get used to it fast, *pethi mou*. I spend my life being stared at.'

Other couples joined them on the dance floor and Sebastien suddenly realized that she was barely moving in his arms. Instead she was holding on to him tightly as if he were the only solid, dependable thing in her life. *As if she were afraid of letting him go*.

He frowned down at the blonde head which was only inches away from his chest.

Where did it come from, this vulnerability that flowed from her?

His mouth hardened as he reminded himself forcibly that this marriage had come about because she didn't have a principled bone in her body. If she seemed vulnerable then it was probably all part of an elaborate act to attract wealthy men.

The truth was that she was a ruthless, manipulative woman, who was willing to go to distasteful lengths to swell her already swollen bank account.

'I'm not letting go,' he drawled lazily, wondering why she was always so conscious of people staring. Having been on the receiving end of public attention since he'd outgrown the privacy of his pram, it was something he no longer noticed. Surely she was the same? 'You signed on for this when you agreed to marry for money.'

Her eyes held a hint of reproach. 'I *didn't* sign on for public performances—'

'You agreed to be my wife,' he responded smoothly, 'with all that entails. Do you know what I think, *pethi mou*? I think you were so blinded by the money you didn't see the rest of it. I don't think you thought further than the cash.'

He felt her stiffen.

He could see a tiny pulse beating in her throat, feel the extraordinary tension throbbing from her delicious body and his own body tightened in an instantaneous response that almost made him groan aloud.

How could he ever have thought that the Philipos heiress was cold?

English and reserved though she may be on the surface, there was now no doubt in his mind that she had enough hot-blooded Greek blood in her to ensure that their sex life would be far from boring.

His head bent lower, his mouth so close to hers that they were almost touching. 'You've got what you wanted. The cheque. Now it's my turn.'

She was staring at him like an animal in a trap. 'You got what you wanted too—my grandfather's company.'

'*My* father's company,' Sebastien corrected her softly, his free hand sliding up her spine and settling on the back of her neck. 'And that was only part of what I wanted. Now it's time to help myself to the rest.'

His gaze mocking, he dipped his head with lazy arrogance and claimed the mouth that had been tempting him ever since she'd first set foot on the island, intending to demonstrate to the Philipos heiress just *exactly* what she'd let herself in for when she'd traded herself for money. Intending to show her that greed had a price.

Her mouth was warm and sweet and his senses exploded, propelling him out of control.

Heat and fire spread through his lower body and he was consumed by a sexual need so powerful that he dragged her closer still in an attempt to satisfy the sudden grinding ache in his loins, but the action simply inflamed him still further.

They were so close that he felt every tiny tremor of her body, felt her shiver as he held her. He saw the shock in her violet eyes before they drifted shut and her fingers curled into the front of his shirt for support.

His last coherent thought was that *this* wasn't what he'd planned.

A small part of his brain told him to pull away, to end it now, but her soft, delicious mouth drugged his senses and prevented him from doing anything except help himself to more.

He filled himself with her. The scent of her slithered over him like a suffocating cloak, the blood in his head raged and pounded, clouding thought and reason. Lust ravaged his body as he plunged into a raging heat totally new to him. The fire burned red then gold and he fanned the flames by taking more and more of her.

As if from a distance he heard a soft whimper of shock and desire and that tiny sound was enough to break the sensual spell that she'd wrapped around him.

He dragged his mouth from hers with supreme difficulty, discovering for the first time what it felt like to be completely out of control.

What the hell was he playing at?

He'd always considered himself to be a ruthlessly disciplined man. Whatever the situation, be it provocation or temptation, he *never* lost control. *So why, once his mouth had taken possession of hers, had he suddenly lost all ability to think rationally?* In fact he'd stopped thinking altogether, his actions driven by an instinct so raw and primitive that he'd been well past control.

His body still hummed with unfulfilled tension, his nerves sizzled and his manhood ached and throbbed.

The realization that she'd succeeded in affecting him so strongly irritated him in the extreme and he struggled to rationalize his own behaviour. To find some explanation for such an uncharacteristic reaction.

Was it really so surprising? he wondered, surveying her flushed, shocked face with grim concentration.

Whatever else she may be, there was no denying that his new wife was a stunningly beautiful woman who managed to project just the right amount of innocence and vulnerability to tempt a very traditionally minded Greek male.

He wouldn't be human if he didn't respond.

And the cure was to take her to bed, he decided with characteristic decisiveness. Women, however beautiful, never held his attention for long. One night, maybe two, would be all it would take to get his fill of her. After that he'd be able to start thinking clearly again and move on.

Decision made, he grabbed Alesia's wrist and virtually hauled her off the dance floor towards the exit without uttering a word.

And just to be sure that the staring guests were left in no doubt as to how he felt about his new bride, he swept her up into his arms and planted another swift kiss on her shocked mouth.

With a smile at his mother, who was shedding tears of undisguised delight on the arm of his father, he strode out of the garden towards the waiting limousine.

Alesia didn't wriggle in his arms, didn't move. It was almost as if she wanted him to take her away from there. Which couldn't possibly be the case, he reflected grimly, because another thing he knew about women was that the whole point of spend, spend, spend was to allow them to party, party, party.

Her head lay against his shoulder in almost weary resignation and he felt something pull inside him. *A feeling which he instantly dismissed with a sharp frown.*

She was good, he had to hand it to her. She was already trying to tie him in knots. A less experienced man might have thought that she was glad he was holding her.

Fortunately he knew better—

One night, he promised himself as he dropped her in the seat of the limo as if she was infectious.

He'd make her pregnant that first night and that would be it.

He wouldn't have to touch her again.

He could get on with his life and she could get on with spending his money.

CHAPTER FOUR

ALESIA huddled into the leather seat, trying to control the tiny tremors that still attacked her body. Sebastien's skilled assault on her senses had left her shattered by the discovery that she didn't know herself at all.

Stunned by her own reaction, she struggled to rationalize what had happened.

Nothing had prepared her for that kiss.

It had been dark, terrifying, *exciting* and he'd unveiled a part of herself that she hadn't known existed.

Everything about her felt different.

She wanted to lift her fingers to her lips and see what had changed but she didn't dare with him seated beside her.

She didn't want him to know what he'd done to her—

What he'd made her feel—

She closed her eyes and gave a whimper of self-disgust. What an irony. She'd kissed men before and felt nothing. Why was it that the first man to show her what a kiss could mean had to be a man she despised?

'You can open your eyes now.' Sebastien sounded bored, as if he'd rather be anywhere than sitting next to her. 'We've left the crowds behind. It's just you and me. No more pretending.'

Still struggling with the humiliating knowledge that she hadn't even tried to push him away, Alesia opened her eyes and swallowed hard.

'Where exactly are we going?' Her voice was a nervous croak and he gave a grim smile.

'Somewhere more private. The time has come to take our

''business deal'' to another level, *pethi mou*, and for that I do *not* need an audience.'

How could he speak like that when he clearly wished he were with anyone but her? How could he even be contemplating spending the night with her?

Suddenly she understood the true meaning of the phrase 'out of the frying-pan into the fire' and wished they were back at the reception. She'd thought that being in crowds of people was bad but it was nothing compared to being alone with Sebastien Fiorukis. 'Is it far? I'm very tired—'

'We're going to my Athens home,' he returned, shrugging off his jacket and removing his tie. 'And it isn't far. But you won't be sleeping, *pethi mou*, no matter how exhausted you are. You still have the rest of your bargain to keep. And after that kiss I think we're both going to have a *very* interesting evening.'

His blunt reminder of what they'd shared sent tingles through her already sensitized body and a slow, insidious warmth uncurled low in her pelvis. Desire, hot, restless and totally unfamiliar, tangled and pumped inside her.

She saw the sardonic gleam in his black eyes and swallowed hard. 'I don't know what you mean—'

'No?' Sebastien was hard, tough and uncompromising but his voice was silky smooth as he undid the top few buttons of his shirt. 'Need a reminder?'

Dark hairs nestled in the dip of his bronzed throat, a tantalizing hint of what he kept concealed.

Alesia flattened herself in the furthest corner of the car, enveloped by a sudden rush of panic and something altogether more complicated that she couldn't begin to name.

Up until this moment she hadn't even considered Sebastien as a man. She'd seen him as the enemy and as the answer to her mother's problems. Never as a man.

Until that kiss.

The kiss had wakened something in her. Taken her by storm. *Changed her.*

Suddenly she was aware of him as a man. *And for the first time in her life she was aware of herself as a woman.*

Like a rabbit in a trap, she stared at him. He lounged with careless ease in the seat next to her, long legs stretched out in front of him, an air of almost bored indifference on his handsome face. It was the first time she'd seen him anything less than rigidly formal and her eyes were drawn first to his powerful shoulders, the strong line of his hard jaw, blue-black with stubble.

She realized with a sudden lurch of her stomach that the trappings of wealth and success disguised the essence of the man he was. Underneath his sophisticated exterior lay man at his most primitive and basic. Dark and dangerous. Raw and untamed. *A hunter.* She was just contemplating what that meant for her when she realized that they'd driven through electric gates and were approaching a large and very beautiful villa set in acres of grounds.

Momentarily distracted, she just gazed in silence. 'It's *huge*,' she mumbled finally. 'And there's only one of you.'

He gave a short laugh. 'And, as you've just discovered, I have an extremely large extended family,' he said drily, 'all of whom frequently decide to descend on me at once and need to be accommodated. I also do a great deal of business entertaining. I need the space.'

Alesia stared at him in disbelief and then back at the house. He needed this much space? She was used to living in a room where she could virtually touch all four walls from her bed.

'I hope the house comes with a map,' she muttered as she stepped out of the car. Immediately she realized her mistake as Sebastien stared at her with brooding concentration.

'You are the granddaughter of a man who is richer than Midas. Your grandfather is well-known for keeping elaborate homes. Why would you be so surprised at mine?'

Alesia bit her tongue.

She'd slipped up again.

Stupid stupid stupid.

Warning herself that she *had* to concentrate, she tried to recover her mistake.

'I've never been that great at finding my way around new places,' she muttered vaguely as he took her arm and led her towards the door.

'Fortunately there's only one room that you need to find,' he advised in cool tones, 'and that's the bedroom.'

Alesia flushed to the roots of her glossy blonde hair and would have stopped walking but he swept her up in his arms and carried her across a spacious marble hallway and up a beautifully curved staircase.

'I can walk—' she said through gritted teeth and he flashed her a grim smile.

'This isn't for your benefit, *agape mou*, but for the benefit of my staff who are at this moment peeping discreetly round corners hoping for a glimpse of my new bride. Unfortunately for us, they are as romantically inclined as my mother so I intend to give them the show they're expecting.'

Staff?

Her mouth fell open and she closed it again quickly. Of course a man like him would have staff. How else could he run a house on this scale?

He strode into a room, kicked the door shut behind him and dropped her with little in the way of warning before striding over to the full-length windows and opening them.

His need for fresh air and distance caused a shaft of pain that she couldn't decipher.

So the 'show' was over, she thought wryly, struggling to regain her balance and maintain some shred of dignity.

Now what?

Glancing at the tension in those broad shoulders, her heart sank. He certainly did not look lover-like.

'Look—' her voice was weary '—we both know that this whole situation is ridiculous. We don't have to do this—'

'*This* was part of our agreement.'

He turned, his dark eyes glittering with intent. 'What's the matter?' He strolled towards her with all the grace of a jungle animal stalking its prey. 'Having second thoughts? Suddenly realizing what it is you agreed to?'

His tone was clipped and hard and her heart leaped into her throat. Distant, cold and monumentally intimidating, Sebastien was totally out of her league and it was useless pretending otherwise.

'What *we* agreed to,' she corrected, taking a step backwards and then wishing she hadn't as he registered the defensive movement on her part with a cool smile.

'*We* agreed to a marriage,' he reminded her softly, lifting his hands and unbuttoning the rest of his shirt with slow, deliberate flicks of his long fingers, each movement taunting her. 'And that is what we're going to have, *Mrs* Fiorukis.'

He peeled off his shirt and let it fall to the floor with casual disregard. But then he was probably never going to wear it again, Alesia thought hysterically as she took another step back and suddenly realized that there was nowhere else for her to go. Her back was against the wall. Literally.

With considerable difficulty, she moved her gaze from the tantalizing vision of bronzed skin and rough chest hair clustered against rock-solid muscle. Heart thudding hard, mouth dry, she stared defiantly into the corner of the room, just *refusing* to look at him. Perhaps if she didn't look, then she wouldn't feel. *Wouldn't want.*

The sound of a zip being undone made her flinch, the rustle of silk sliding to the floor made her nerve-endings tingle, and at that point she closed her eyes, just *knowing* that he was naked and absolutely determined not to look.

'Well, Mrs Fiorukis?' His rough masculine voice taunted

her and she sensed him moving closer. *And closer.* 'Are you ready to close this particular part of the deal?'

Eyes still closed, heart still hammering, she tried to reason with him. 'You can't possibly want me and I *certainly* don't want you—'

He was too close.

His raw masculine scent surrounded her and oozed into her senses, making her stomach drop and her legs weaken.

'On the contrary, I paid an indecent sum of money for you,' he reminded her coldly, 'and I expect you to earn that money.'

Her eyes flew open and she gave a disbelieving laugh. 'In the bedroom?'

'Where else?' He gave a bored shrug. 'I'm certainly not in need of your assistance in the boardroom.'

Her mind searched frantically for an escape from the building sexual tension which was threatening her ability to think or function.

'You already have a mistress—'

'Several,' he confirmed helpfully, 'but you needn't worry that it will affect my performance in bed.'

She didn't even want to think about bed.

Every inch of her throbbed. Her senses danced and pirouetted in a crazy response to the man in front of her.

'Look—I'm trying to be honest,' she said desperately, 'and the truth is we just don't have to do this. You can go to your mistress—I don't care—'

She didn't need this. Didn't want this. She wanted freedom from these feelings that she didn't recognize. Hadn't felt before.

'But my mistress won't give me children,' he reminded her silkily, 'and I want children. And *this* is the way children are made, remember?'

Her gaze, showing a glimmer of guilt, flew to his. It was a mistake. Slumberous dark eyes captured and trapped her, drawing her in. Those eyes alone were enough to make a woman lose herself, she thought dizzily, struggling to remember why it was that she didn't want to go to bed with him. His eyelashes were long and dark and ridiculously thick and his hard jaw was covered in blue-black stubble that made him look even more dangerous.

'If you're nervous then you needn't be,' he said. 'I may not like you but that kiss alone was enough to prove to both of us that, despite our emotions, physically at least there is a powerful chemistry between us.'

Alesia felt dizzy and drugged and her mouth was so dry she could barely speak.

She gaped at him. 'Chemistry? You think there's chemistry between us?'

'I know there is—' he curved a hand round her waist and drew her against him '—and so do you. Stop pretending you don't feel it too.'

Alesia was so busy trying to understand his belief that there was chemistry between them that she somehow managed to miss the fact that his hand was moving down her back. With a swift, purposeful movement he undid her dress and she gave a soft gasp of shock as it pooled at her feet, leaving her dressed in only a pair of silk panties.

Consumed by embarrassment, she lifted her arms to cover her naked breasts but Sebastien caught her hands and drew them around his neck before scooping her up in his arms.

'This is definitely *not* the time to cover up your best assets,' he urged thickly, carrying her to the bed and depositing her in the centre.

Before she could move a muscle, he came down on top of her, his weight pinning her to the bed.

'Whatever your faults, you have a *fabulous* body,' he said huskily, sliding a lean bronzed hand over her body with maddening slowness as he surveyed her with raw male appreciation. 'I'll be honest about one thing, *pethi mou*, I was all ready to refuse this deal whatever the incentive and then I saw you.'

Her breath jammed in her throat. 'You were going to refuse?'

'Of course.' He raised his head to look at her and there was a flicker of dry amusement in his dark eyes. 'We are expected to make babies for our respective families, *agape mou*, and that requires a certain activity on my part. If I had found you unattractive there was no way I would have agreed to this marriage. Despite rumours to the contrary, I'm *extremely* particular about who I take to my bed.'

She stared up at him, her heart pounding, her resistance crumbling to dust under the hot sexuality of his gaze. 'You find me attractive—really?'

No man had ever looked twice at her before but then she'd gone out of her way to avoid all but platonic relationships with the opposite sex.

'Really.' His tone of self-mockery drew her attention to his body for the first time and her colour deepened. It was the first time she'd seen a naked man. A naked aroused man. The sight was nothing short of daunting.

Now that the moment had come, panic assailed her. He was right, she thought, closing her eyes with a helpless moan as his mouth traced the line of her jaw. She hadn't really thought this through. How could she ever have thought she'd be able to pretend that she was experienced? She didn't have a *clue* and there was no way she'd ever be able to convince him otherwise.

'You loathe me,' she moaned, moving her head away from his clever mouth with a gasp of disbelief. 'You despise me. You can't possibly want me.'

She was wondering frantically what to do when Sebastien took control and, with a smooth shift of his powerful frame, he rolled her under him and lowered his mouth to hers. Instantly her body erupted and with a whimper of helpless excitement she realized that he was so used to being in charge that all she had to do was to lie there and he'd make all the moves. He'd show her the way.

It was her last logical thought before she fell deep into his kiss—

Just like the time before, she forgot everything. She felt the erotic slide of his tongue in her mouth, the hotly sexual exploration that sent shivers through her whole body and had her arching against him. She felt his hand move downwards, dragging over one sensitized nipple and resting on her hip.

And her head started to spin. Nothing felt straight or clear.

Her heart hammered, her pelvis burned and her senses tangled and swirled in an exotic dance, fired by the sensual thrust of his tongue.

Just when she thought she was definitely going to pass out, he dragged his mouth away from hers. With a reluctant groan he trailed his mouth down over her neck, her throat, until finally he lingered on her breast.

At the first casual flick of his tongue she cried out in shock, driven wild by the intensity of the sensation, and as he sucked her into his mouth she shifted her hips in a desperate attempt to soothe the wild burning in her pelvis.

'You have amazing breasts,' he groaned, turning his attention to the other one. 'It was virtually the only thing I noticed about you when we first met.'

Some deeper part of her brain registered that remark but she wasn't capable of any reaction other than a pleading whimper.

She wanted more—*something*—

'Sebastien—' She breathed his name on a sob of desperation and he gave a wolfish smile of male triumph.

'And the other thing I like about you,' he murmured huskily as he slid further down her frantically writhing and excited body, 'is that underneath that prim, restrained exterior you are *so* hot. How could I ever have thought that you were cold and English?'

Alesia couldn't even respond because at that moment he spread her legs in a ruthlessly possessive gesture and concentrated his attentions on an entirely different part of her body.

Torn between shock at being exposed to a man's gaze for the first time and a sensual pleasure so terrifying in its intensity that she could hardly breathe let alone think, Alesia bit back a moan of denial. Resisting her feeble attempts to close her legs, he held her firm and used his tongue with an erotic mastery that made her writhe and sob in an ecstasy that she hadn't even dreamed existed before this moment. She just couldn't believe that he was doing these things to her and that she was *encouraging* him.

'Sebastien—' Confused and overwhelmed by the sudden explosion of sexual need that she didn't properly understand, she arched her back and curled her fingers into the sheets. *'Sebastien—'*

He slid up the bed in a fluid movement, his eyes scanning her flushed cheeks with ill-disguised satisfaction. 'Definitely *not* cold,' he murmured, his hand closing over her wrist as she reached to pull the sheet up. 'No way. You never cover up until I say so and I haven't finished looking at you yet.'

His gaze made her feel hotter still and he slid a hair-roughened thigh over her legs as she writhed against the sheets in an attempt to relieve the burning need that threatened to consume her whole body.

'Something the matter?' he taunted her softly, his eyes shimmering dark with barely restrained passion. 'Is there something you want from me other than my money, *agape mou*?'

Her body throbbed and ached from his all too skilled seduction and she was just *desperate* for him to finish what he'd started.

'Say it,' he said harshly, shifting his weight so that his powerful body covered hers, teasing her further. She felt his silken arousal hard against her and curled her legs round him, arching in mute invitation.

Still he held himself back, his gaze faintly mocking as he looked down at her.

'Lose that English reserve. Tell me what you want, *agape mou*,' he commanded and she lay looking up at him, totally in his control, her heart beating rapidly and her body consumed by a powerful craving that she just had to satisfy.

'You,' she groaned softly, writhing under him in a wanton attempt to get closer. 'You. I want you. *Please*.'

With a growl of masculine satisfaction, Sebastien slid an arm under her hips, lifted her in a decisive movement and thrust into her with barely restrained masculine force.

Shocked by the power of that alien invasion, Alesia gave a sharp cry and her eyes flew wide and clashed with his.

She saw the sudden speculation in his sultry, sexy gaze and kept her expression blank. She didn't want him to know. The brief pain faded, extinguished by her driving need for physical satisfaction, and she moved her hips under his. His eyes still holding hers, he lowered his head and captured her mouth, teasing and tasting with his tongue until her whole body was burning hot and writhing under his.

Only then did he move again, this time incredibly gently as if he was trying not to hurt her. And his unexpected tenderness made the whole experience unbearably erotic. Alesia clutched at his broad shoulders and slid her hands down his muscular back, feeling the degree of strength and power that he'd so carefully leashed on her account.

Without moving his mouth from hers, he lifted her with a strong arm, shifting her position, and ripples of excitement exploded through her sensitized body as he changed the angle.

How did he know?

How did he know to move in a certain way, touch her in a certain way?

How could he make her feel like this?

She gasped his name against his mouth and he gave a growl of satisfaction low in his throat and thrust hard, each stroke long and deep as he controlled her and drove her to completion. She shot into orgasm with a strangled cry of disbelief, her body convulsing around his in waves and waves of pulsing ecstasy that refused to end.

It was wild and uninhibited and totally outside her control, her body just exploding in a frenzy of raw sexual excitement.

She heard him mutter something rough in Greek and then with a harsh groan he grabbed her hips and buried himself deeper still, not even giving her a chance to escape from the storm that was overtaking them.

She felt his hardness and his heat and then felt his muscles bunch as her frantic convulsions propelled him to his own climax. She felt his fingers dig into her scalp, felt the liquid pulse of his release as he powered into her, driven over the edge by the living force they'd created between them.

Locked in the throes of pleasure which refused to diminish, Alesia slid a hand over his muscled back, feeling the heat of his skin, the vital masculinity of the man, as he struggled to control his breathing.

His weight crushed her to the bed, his body still locked with hers in the most intimate way possible, and it crossed her mind that this was the closest she'd ever felt to anyone in her life. They were connected in every sense of the word.

For a long moment Alesia lay still, utterly stunned by what had happened.

Never in her wildest dreams or fantasies had she imagined that it would be like that.

That two human beings could be so close.

With a brief frown of confusion she lifted a hand hesitantly and touched his bronzed shoulder.

What had happened?

She'd started out hating him, and now—

She swallowed hard and tried to make sense of what had just happened. Sifting through her tangled emotions, suddenly she couldn't find the hatred any more. How could you share such intimacies with someone and hate them?

And surely he couldn't hate her, either? How could something so perfect have been created out of hate? It wasn't possible—

She felt something inside her melt away, leaving her exposed and vulnerable but she didn't care. She'd discovered something that she hadn't known existed. Something amazing.

Guilt and confusion mingled inside her. They'd shared something really honest and yet she'd told him such *lies*. What would he say if he knew the extent to which she was deceiving him?

Maybe she should tell him—

After what they'd shared, she needed to be honest.

Sebastien lifted his dark head and stared down at her flushed cheeks and bruised mouth for a long moment. Then he rolled on to his back and covered his face with a bronzed forearm.

Feeling suddenly awkward, Alesia lay still, suddenly impossibly shy, not wanting to be the first to speak. For a short time they'd been as close as two people could be. They'd shared something special and the whole world had shifted. Everything seemed different. He *had* to feel it too.

They had to speak about it. *She had to tell him the truth.* Surely he'd say something in a moment.

'It looks as though I'm going to get my money's worth.' His tone was cool and matter-of-fact.

Without so much as a glance in her direction, he sprang

out of bed with the lithe grace of a jungle cat and strolled
into the bathroom, slamming the door behind him, leaving
her rigid with shock.

Sebastien stood under the shower trying to recover from what
had proved to be the most explosive sexual encounter of his
entire life. His usually sharp mind was foggy and his body
throbbed in a state of almost agonized arousal. Breathing
heavily, he eyed the door of the bathroom, torn between a
primitive need to satisfy his libido and a desire to regain
some sort of control over his unusually scattered emotions.

He wasn't used to feeling like this.

With an exclamation of disbelief he thumped the button
on the wall and turned the water into an icy blast. He gritted
his teeth and let the water sluice over his thoroughly over-
heated body, seeking relief from his state of almost intolerable discomfort.

It was either that or return to the bed and make love to
her again and again and again and that *wasn't* what this marriage was about.

He hadn't expected to derive much pleasure from the experience.

Irritated beyond belief by her total obsession with money,
he'd taken her to bed to make her feel cheap, to see if he
could trigger any signs of conscience.

He hadn't expected her reaction to him to be so totally
uninhibited. Hadn't expected the chemistry between them to
be so powerful.

And he hadn't expected her to be a virgin.

Cursing fluently he turned off the water, swept a bronzed
hand over his face to clear his vision and reached for a towel.
He was a man who was used to always being in control and
while he'd been in bed with Alesia he *definitely* hadn't been.
The knowledge that his loss of control had been with a
woman whose values he despised made his response even
more reprehensible in his opinion.

Or did it? Was it really so surprising that he'd found the encounter almost unbelievably erotic? he wondered. The women he usually spent time with moved in the same circles as him, were sophisticated and sexually experienced. Sebastien gave a wry smile of self-mockery as he wrapped the towel around his lean hips. At what point had he lost sight of the truth? That, when all was said and done, he was, in fact, a *very* traditional Greek male and like all traditional men he preferred exclusivity when it came to women.

It hadn't occurred to him that his new wife might be a virgin and the truth was that her innocence in the bedroom had somehow served to heighten the emotional and physical experience. Given that it wasn't an encounter he intended to repeat in the near future, he didn't need to worry.

Having rationalized his response to his satisfaction, Sebastien glanced warily at the door that led to the bedroom.

He'd get on with his own life, leaving her to spend his money. And if she wasn't already pregnant then he'd sleep with her again at some point.

It was a good job that he was likely to be kept extremely busy for the foreseeable future.

Alesia lay still, eyes tightly closed, physically drained and enveloped by a humiliation so acute that she could barely bring herself to address what had happened.

How could he be so *hurtful*?

And to think she'd almost told him the truth.

She groaned as she remembered her own reaction to him. *She'd had no idea it would be like that.* That she was capable of such intensity of feeling. None of the limited experience she'd had before had prepared her for such a scenario.

How could she have responded so wildly to a man that she didn't even *like*?

She covered her face with her arms.

And how was she ever going to look him in the face again?

For him it had clearly just been sex, whereas for her—
Remembering how she'd sobbed his name and virtually
begged, she gave another whimper of disbelief. There was
no escaping the fact that she'd inadvertently given him yet
more ammunition to feed his already monumental ego.

She lay in the bed, listening to the sound of the shower,
dreading the moment when the water stopped. She didn't
want to be here when he came back. *Didn't want to give him
the chance to humiliate her still further.*

But before she could move the bathroom door opened and
he strolled out, wearing nothing but a narrow towel tucked
loosely around his lean hips.

Now what?

Was he planning on returning to the marital bed?

Against her will, her eyes fastened on the dark hair on his
chest and travelled downwards, knowing exactly what exciting secrets the towel concealed.

Her mouth dried and she felt the immediate response of
her own body.

She ached in places she'd never ached before and when
he casually dropped the towel on the floor and strolled towards her, a vision of bronzed, masculine perfection, her
heart thundered in delicious anticipation.

Unable to drag her eyes away from his magnificent body,
Alesia struggled to breathe. How could she not have noticed
before how staggeringly good-looking he was?

And how could he be so relaxed and at ease when her
entire body was humming with tension?

Didn't he feel it too?

He strolled to the edge of the bed, cast her a sweeping
glance from under thick black lashes and then reached for
his Rolex which he'd left on the bedside table.

It was only when he turned away from her that she realized
she'd been holding her breath.

She stared at him as he walked back across the room and

started to dress and the question spilled out before she could stop it. 'Are you coming back to bed?'

'For what purpose?' His tone was bored and he didn't even glance in her direction as he finished dressing. 'This was business, remember, and for now at least that part of our business is concluded.'

'And that's it?' Her voice was barely a whisper as she sat up, clutching the silk sheets to her breasts. 'That's all you're going to say?'

He paused in the doorway, his lean, strong face displaying not one flicker of emotion as he studied her in brooding contemplation. 'Let me know if you're pregnant.'

With that he strolled out of the room and let the door swing closed behind him.

Soaked in humiliation, Alesia sank back against the pillows.

How could he be so totally cold and unfeeling? Such an utter bastard?

Almost screaming with anger and frustration, she rolled over to try and ease the maddening ache in her body and gritted her teeth.

It didn't matter what he said or how he touched her, she was *never* letting him back in her bed again!

CHAPTER FIVE

Two weeks later Alesia was in the enormous kitchen at the far end of the house when Sebastien came striding into the room, simmering with barely restrained masculine aggression, a thunderous look on his handsome face.

'What the *hell* are you doing in here?' In raw frustration he raked lean bronzed fingers through sleek, dark hair and inhaled deeply. 'I have been searching *everywhere* for you. No one had a clue where you were.'

Sexual awareness shot through her body and Alesia dug her nails into her palms.

Two weeks.

It had been two whole weeks since she'd last laid eyes on him and, like a young puppy seeing his master after a long separation, her quivering, yearning body just exploded with excitement.

One greedy, tentative glance at that lean, handsome face with its fierce, dark eyes and blue-shadowed jaw was enough to make Alesia's stomach drop and her pulse rate double. One glance and she remembered every frantic, hot, seductive moment of the way this man made love. And, if that wasn't bad enough, her whole being just lifted with happiness because he was finally, finally *home*.

Appalled by the strength of her reaction to him, she turned towards the fridge, hiding her face. She couldn't help the way she felt about him but at least she refused to give him the satisfaction of showing him, she thought grimly. He'd already made his thoughts on the subject clear, having slept with her once and then absented himself for two whole weeks. Clearly their one sexual encounter had bored him in the extreme, whereas her complete lack of experience and sophistication meant that she'd left him in no doubt whatsoever that he was a God in the bedroom. The knowledge that she'd held nothing back made her *squirm* with bone-deep humiliation.

She wished she could put the clock back. Two weeks ago she hadn't even noticed his firm, sexy mouth, the seductive glint in his Mediterranean dark eyes or the perfect musculature of his powerful body. She hadn't noticed the superb bone structure or the slightly cynical smile that turned heads everywhere he went. *She hadn't noticed him as a man.* Now she noticed *everything* and every feminine part of her shrieked in recognition of his raw, untamed masculinity.

'Naturally I didn't know that you were searching for me,' she said coolly, poking around in the fridge until she was confident that her betraying colour had subsided. Only when she was sure that she was in control did she remove some cheese and a bowl of glossy dark olives from the fridge and place them on the table. 'And in answer to your question, I'm making myself lunch.'

He strolled into the room and glanced at her with naked incredulity. 'Why?'

Because she'd never had access to so much delicious food in her life and it was just marvellous not to go hungry in order to save money.

She shrugged. 'Why not?'

'Because I have an extensive and well-rewarded staff,' he said slowly, enunciating his words as if he were addressing a child, his astonishment palpable, 'and their job is to produce meals for you so that you don't have to take an inconvenient break in your shopping schedule.'

She flinched at his cutting remark. His opinion of her was just *so* low. But could she really blame him for that? After all, she was the one who'd given him that impression and had to continue to do so. 'I have all the time I need to shop,' she said idly, 'given that I haven't seen you since our wedding day. And your staff have got better things to do than make me lunch.'

He was looking at her with a stunned expression on his handsome face.

'I don't know why you're looking at me like that.' She glanced impatiently in his direction. 'Have you never made yourself lunch before?'

'Frankly, no,' he confessed drily, a strange expression in his eyes as he looked at her. 'And I hadn't exactly expected you to either. Do you often waltz into your grandfather's kitchen and make yourself lunch?'

Alesia froze. She'd done it again. Had forgotten that she was supposed to be rich and pampered. Then she gave a mental shrug.

'I don't expect people to wait on me.' Aware that he was looking at her curiously, she sighed and rolled her eyes. 'Now what?'

'It's just that you constantly surprise me,' he drawled softly, his gaze speculative. 'Just when I think I have you all worked out, you do something that is totally out of character.'

She cast him a look of contempt. 'You know *nothing* about my character.'

'Evidently not,' he murmured, his shimmering dark eyes narrowed as he surveyed her thoughtfully. 'However, I think our staff might be a little shocked if they discover you in here, making lunch.'

Alesia bit her lip and refrained from telling him that she was already on first-name terms with his head chef and that they'd swapped Greek and English recipes. 'They're *your* staff.'

'You're *my* wife.'

Her body tingled at his silky reminder. 'Forgive me for forgetting that fact,' she said acidly. 'I haven't seen you since our wedding day two weeks ago. I assumed you'd taken up residence elsewhere.'

And she just *hated* him for not even bothering to show his face.

'I didn't realize you were going to miss me so much and it was our wedding *night*,' he corrected softly, studying her through narrowed eyes. 'You saw me on our wedding night. Another occasion when you surprised me. I wasn't expecting a virgin in my bed.'

Her cheeks flamed. 'I don't know what you mean—'

'You should have told me,' he said smoothly. 'Greek men are very possessive, *agape mou*. I might have been prepared to raise the purchase price still further had I realized the unique value of the goods. You missed out.'

She winced at his mercenary assessment of her character. 'I was satisfied with the deal.'

His eyes glittered in his handsome face. 'I'm beginning to think that I might be too,' he drawled, stepping closer to her. 'You were *amazingly* responsive.'

Graphic images flashed through her brain and her legs started to tremble as the memories came crashing back.

'You paid me to perform in your bed,' she said unsteadily, 'so that's what I did.'

He gave a short laugh and moved closer still. 'You were *totally* out of control, *agape mou*, and you expect me to believe that you were acting?'

He was too close. She couldn't breathe. *Couldn't think.*

She wasn't used to dealing with men like him. She wasn't used to talking about sex.

Careful not to look at him, she sliced the cheese into chunks and laid it in a bowl. 'It wasn't my choice to introduce sex into our marriage. I was perfectly happy to have a very different sort of marriage.'

'One where I pay you to do nothing?'

'You weren't paying me for sex,' she said steadily, adding

olives to the bowl. 'You were paying me for the ''privilege'' of taking over my grandfather's company.'

'It might interest you to know that that particular ''privilege'' has taken up every daylight hour since our wedding,' he drawled, his eyes raking over her in frowning contemplation. 'Your grandfather is an appalling businessman. You can blame him for the fact that you haven't seen me.'

'I'd rather thank him,' she said, putting the finishing touches to her salad and lifting the bowl. 'I had no desire to spend any time with you at all. And now, if you'll excuse me, I'm planning to go and eat my lunch.'

And phone her mother.

That had been one of the major benefits of Sebastien's long absence. She'd been in daily contact and was following her mother's progress anxiously.

'No.' His voice was lethally soft as he lifted the bowl from her clutching fingers and returned it to the table. 'I do *not* excuse you.'

She made the mistake of looking at him. Stormy blue eyes clashed with smouldering black and instantly the breath caught in her chest.

The look in his eyes was intensely sexual and she could see that his mind most certainly wasn't on anything as boring as lunch.

His eyes moved from hers, lingering on the full curve of her breasts and then sliding down to rest on her smooth, flat stomach exposed by her hipster jeans. 'Don't wear trousers again. You have great legs. I want to see them—'

'You are such a chauvinist,' she flung at him, her cheeks flaming with colour at his remark. 'Do you always tell women what to wear?'

'Women don't usually go out with me looking as though they're about to unblock a drain.'

'I like my jeans. They're comfortable.'

'So is underwear,' he said silkily, his lashes lowering as

he gave her a look of pure sexual speculation. 'And that would be my preference.'

Knees shaking, she put a hand on the table for support. 'I'll wear what I want to wear—'

'Not in my company,' he said, his tone suddenly icy. 'You'll wear what I want to see you in.'

She bit her lip. 'That's ridiculous.'

'You should have thought of that before you sold yourself.'

She gave him an incredulous look. 'You want me wander round your house in my underwear?'

'If I tell you to.' His gaze was mocking. 'I pay enough for you. I might as well see what I'm buying.'

She turned her head so he wouldn't see the tears that stung her eyes. He made her feel so *cheap*. 'Fine.' Pulling herself together, she threw him a tight smile. 'I'll wear my jeans when you're not here, which is most of the time, fortunately. Now, if you don't mind, I'd like to eat my lunch.'

Before she could guess his intention, he curved a lean brown hand around the strip of flesh exposed by her top and hauled her against him.

Trapped by the expression in his eyes, her heart began to hammer against her chest and her head swam alarmingly.

He lifted lean bronzed hands and cupped her face, forcing her to look at him. 'Are you pregnant?'

The question threw her and she gazed up at him in total shock. 'No.'

'Good.' He gave a devilish smile and scooped her into his arms. 'And you know what they say—if at first you don't succeed—'

'What are you doing?' She started to wriggle out of his arms but then his mouth fastened on hers in the most erotic kiss imaginable and, like a starving man finally facing the prospect of a meal, she sobbed with relief and fell into that kiss.

His tongue delved into her mouth in an explicit gesture of masculine intent that sent her pulse racing and her head spinning. Her arms slid round his strong neck, her fingers tangled with his silky dark hair and she wriggled in his arms just desperate for more.

Mouths locked, they ravaged each other, biting, licking, exchanging gasps and groans, stoking the heat between them to almost intolerable levels.

His mouth still fastened to hers, he lowered her back to the ground and thrust her back against the wall, every inch of his powerful body hard against hers.

Alesia sucked in some much-needed air, her stomach tumbling frantically as she felt the heavy throb of his arousal against her.

A sound in the corridor outside made them both freeze.

'*Theos mou*, what are we doing?' He glanced around him in naked disbelief. 'This is my *kitchen*, a room I have only visited a few times in my whole life.'

She closed her eyes in embarrassment. 'Someone could have walked in—'

'No chance. If they had I would have fired them,' Sebastien announced raggedly, closing long fingers around her wrist and virtually dragging her out of the room. 'I value my privacy above everything else and my staff are fully aware of that fact.'

Hoping the staff in question were nowhere nearby to witness her surrender to caveman tactics, Alesia struggled to keep up with his long stride. 'Where are we going?'

'Somewhere I will not have to stare at pots and pans when I have finished with you,' he said silkily, striding towards the stairs so rapidly that she virtually had to run to keep up with him.

'*Sebastien—*'

Once in the bedroom he kicked the door shut behind them, lifted her up and deposited her in the middle of his bed.

She'd promised herself that if he ever came near her again she'd slap his arrogant face and walk in the opposite direction. So why was it that she couldn't move?

She watched in hypnotized fascination as he lifted a lean brown hand and removed his tie with a few skilled flicks of those clever fingers. His eyes never leaving hers, he undid the buttons on his shirt and yanked it off, revealing a bronzed muscular chest covered in curling dark hairs.

'Time to lose the jeans,' he suggested helpfully, his shimmering dark gaze fastened on her flushed face as he dispensed with the rest of his clothes with single-minded purpose. 'Do it yourself, or I'll do it for you.'

Alesia lay frozen, helpless to look away from his fabulous body. No wonder he was totally unselfconscious about parading around naked, she thought numbly. He was as near perfect as a man could get and just looking at him made her mouth dry.

Without the outward trappings of sophistication he was revealed in all his masculine glory.

Desire heated and coiled low in her pelvis and her breathing quickened in anticipation.

Lithe and athletic, he came down on the bed next to her, one arm sliding under her and stripping off her clothes in a series of deft, decisive moves.

'That's how I prefer you, *pethi mou*,' he growled, his heated gaze sliding down her naked, trembling length in blatant sexual appraisal.

Alesia squirmed with anticipation and forgot her resolve not to let him touch her again. Every part of her burned for him and the worst thing was that he knew it. He gave a low, satisfied laugh and teased the tip of one breast with slow flicks of his tongue.

She gasped and arched towards him and he answered her unspoken plea for more by sliding his hand downwards, his strong fingers finding her slick warmth.

He gave a groan of acknowledgement. 'Waiting two weeks clearly has its benefits,' he said hoarsely. 'It's amazingly gratifying to have a wife who is so willing.'

The barely veiled insult went straight over her head and, with a shocking degree of masculine purpose, Sebastien raised her hips and thrust into her hard.

'Is this what you want?' He shifted her position and drove deeper still and Alesia let out a thickened moan, swamped by an almost intolerable sexual excitement.

Her body exploded into orgasm and Sebastien brought his mouth down on hers and kissed her hard, smothering her sobs with the pressure of his mouth and stealing her breath with the intimate lick of his tongue.

He thrust into her with rhythmic force, his powerful body shuddering over hers as he reached his own completion. Finally he dragged his mouth from hers and inhaled unsteadily.

Stormy black eyes clashed with hers and then he rolled on to his side and gathered her against him, curving her slim, trembling body against his powerful frame.

'That was simply amazing,' he said huskily, sliding a leisurely hand down her back and between her legs, 'if a little quick. So now we'll do it again. Slowly.'

Still trembling from the force of her own climax, she gave a gasp of shock which turned to a moan of disbelief and longing as his skilled fingers slid into her already hotly excited body. He stroked and teased her in the most intimate way possible and then rolled her on to her stomach with the supreme confidence of a man with a single purpose in mind.

Battling with the realization that he intended to do it again and that she had no intention of stopping him, Alesia buried her burning face in the pillow and gave a moan of denial as he lifted her on to her knees and positioned himself behind her.

She opened her mouth on a shocked gasp, intending to

protest that he couldn't—*they couldn't*—and then felt the silken pressure of his masculine arousal against her most intimate place. Unconsciously she moved her hips in feminine invitation and heard him mutter something in Greek before his strong hands grasped her writhing hips and anchored her for his powerful thrust.

Alesia went up in flames. Never in her whole life had she ever imagined a sensation so indescribably, unbelievably, *wickedly* good. Still sensitized from her first climax, her body started to contract immediately and she heard him utter a shocked exclamation as she exploded into orgasm within seconds of his penetration.

No longer in control of any part of herself, Alesia cried out and sobbed, begged and moaned, so totally uninhibited and driven by passion that her whole body was a quivering mass of sensation.

She felt the unrestrained power of driving masculine thrusts, heard his hoarse exclamation of disbelief and then lost touch with reality as his own pulsing release sent her over the edge into ecstasy yet again.

For a moment they were both held suspended in a place of such exquisite excitement that reality no longer existed for either of them. And then finally the wildness subsided, leaving them both shuddering in the aftermath of an unbelievable experience.

Eventually Sebastien moved, but only to roll both of them back on to the bed with a very male groan of undiluted sexual satisfaction.

Alesia lay with her eyes closed, shell-shocked and totally exhausted. She couldn't believe that she could have behaved in such a way. Couldn't believe she was capable of being so shameless and abandoned. *And she couldn't believe that it had been even better than last time.* This time she'd known what he was capable of doing to her, what she was capable of feeling, and that knowledge had heightened her excitement to intolerable levels.

'Well, that was definitely an improvement on an afternoon of meetings,' he drawled, his eyes still closed as he lay on his back, one bronzed arm resting across his face, the other holding her firmly against him. 'Had I known how hot you were when I signed those papers I wouldn't have hesitated. You are worth every penny of the money you charge.'

Plunged back into the stark reality of her life by his harsh words, Alesia kept her eyes tightly shut, wishing that he'd stayed in the meetings. At least then she wouldn't have had to cope with the knowledge that she'd once more abandoned herself totally to a man who clearly despised her.

'I don't know how you can make love to me when you so clearly hate me,' she murmured, careful to keep the shake out of her voice as she struggled to forget all the things she'd begged him to do to her while she'd been under the influence of his superior seduction technique.

'Because we don't make love,' he drawled flatly, his eyes hard as they locked with hers. 'We have sex, Alesia. And, fortunately for you, having sex does not require emotional attachment. If it did then men would never use the services of prostitutes.'

She gave a gasp of pain and curled her fingers into the sheets. 'Are you comparing me to a prostitute?'

'Not at all.' He gave her a cool smile and sprang out of bed, lithe and energetic, as if he hadn't just spent an entire afternoon engaged in extremely physical activity. 'You're much more expensive.'

'I really, really hate you, do you know that?' Wounded and humiliated, she curled up in the bed and pulled the sheet over her for protection, consumed by a self-loathing so powerful that the pain of it was almost physical. How could she respond to a man who clearly had absolutely no respect for her? 'I don't want you to come near me again.'

It was said for her benefit as much as his but he merely smiled.

'Yes, you do.' He strolled back to the bed and leaned over, planting both arms on the mattress so that his face was only inches from hers. 'Do you think I don't know how much you ache for me? You may want to hate me but, fortunately for both of us, your hot little body is totally lacking in scruples and the moment I flick the switch you're mine.'

She lifted a hand to slap his face but he caught it with a warning glance.

'Not nice, my little wife,' he purred softly. 'You made your bed and now you're lying in it. Or rather, you're lying in mine. On your front, on your back, whichever way I choose to position you. And that's where you're going to stay.'

Her eyes clouded with pain. 'I want you to leave me alone—'

'Not a chance.' With a final lingering glance at her lush mouth, Sebastien straightened and picked up the phone by the bed, his eyes fixed on hers as he spoke in rapid Greek. Minutes later there was a discreet tap on the door and he answered it and came back to bed carrying a tray. 'Sit up. You need to eat or you'll collapse on me later.'

She stayed stubbornly under the sheet. 'I'm not hungry.'

'We've just had sex without stopping for six hours,' he said in a conversational tone. 'You didn't eat that lunch and you're going to miss dinner. I don't want you fainting on me in the nightclub.'

Six hours? She stared at him in mute astonishment and then glanced at the darkened windows. The knowledge that she'd been so sexually transported that she'd lost all track of time made her want to sink deeper in the bed. It took her a moment to register the rest of his statement.

'Nightclub?' Her voice shook. 'What nightclub—?'

'The one I'm taking you to this evening,' he said smoothly.

'It is a new business venture of a *very* good friend of mine. Athens society will be deciding whether it is the "in" place to be seen.'

And doubtless if Sebastien Fiorukis were there then it would be considered the 'in' place to be seen, she thought helplessly. He was a man who set trends, a man who others followed.

She clutched the sheet. 'I don't feel like going out.'

'Your feelings on the matter are completely irrelevant,' he informed her in a bored tone. 'I wish to make an appearance with my new wife.'

'I'm not getting dressed.'

He didn't hesitate. 'Then I take you naked,' he promised softly, his dark eyes glittering dangerously as he surveyed her. 'It's your decision, *pethi mou*. You're my wife and part of your role is to entertain.'

'I thought I just did,' she said tartly and he gave an appreciative smile.

'That sort of entertainment is for me alone, *agape mou*,' he drawled lazily. 'What I had in mind was something more formal. I am meeting some *very* important guests. I need you to charm them.'

Her jaw lifted stubbornly and she tried a different tack. 'I don't have a single thing to wear—'

He gave the sigh of a male vastly experienced in the challenges presented by female attire. 'On the day of our wedding two weeks ago I furnished you with an indecent sum of money to add to your already *indecent* fortune,' he reminded her in a silky tone. 'Doubtless you have spent the last two entire weeks shopping. Pick something suitable and wear it.'

She swallowed painfully. What was she supposed to say? That she hadn't been near a shop in the two weeks since their wedding?

'I—I haven't bought anything—'

His eyes narrowed and his mouth tightened. 'Every single

penny of the money I gave you has gone from your account,' he said softly. 'You withdrew the whole lot, my hot, sexy wife, so don't tell me that you haven't been spending because I won't believe you.'

Panic slithered over her bones as she realized that he was obviously tracking her spending. How could she have been so naïve as to think he wouldn't know? Did he know where the money had gone? No, or he would have said something.

'I—I bought different things,' she hedged, sitting upright and grabbing at the sheet before it slid to her waist.

With a disbelieving glance in her direction, he prowled into the enormous dressing room that adjoined their bedroom.

Alesia closed her eyes and waited in a state of unbelievable tension for the inevitable explosion.

There was a long, pulsing silence and then he strolled back to the bedroom and picked up the phone again, barking out a set of commands in rapid Greek.

Resolving to learn Greek as soon as possible, Alesia discovered that she was still holding her breath and released it suddenly.

He must have seen that her wardrobes were totally empty and yet he hadn't said a word.

What was going on?

'Use the shower,' he ordered, lifting a bottle of champagne out of an ice bucket and handing it to her. 'By the time you've finished, the clothes will have arrived.'

'What clothes?'

'The clothes I have just ordered for you,' he said with all the casual assurance of someone with a bottomless bank account. She looked at him nervously. Suddenly he seemed very intimidating.

What was she going to say to him when he finally demanded answers on how she'd spent the money?

Her mind in overdrive, searching for plausible excuses, she stumbled into the luxurious bathroom and stood under the revitalizing spray of the shower. Suddenly she had a new awareness of her body and, after five minutes of searing-hot water and several applications of various luxurious shower foams, she realized that nothing was going to wash away the memory of Sebastien's own heady brand of lovemaking.

Filled with a self-loathing that all the water in the world couldn't quench, Alesia turned off the shower, dried herself quickly and wrapped herself in a large fluffy towel that virtually covered her from neck to toe.

Suitably concealed, she lifted her chin and strolled back into the bedroom with as much aloof dignity as she could muster.

Immediately her eyes were drawn to a rail packed with clothes and she stared at the rail and then back at him in amazement. 'Where did these come from? You didn't have time to go to a shop—'

'If you're rich then the shop comes to you,' he informed her smoothly, 'but, as the pampered granddaughter of Dimitrios Philipos, I'm sure you don't need me to tell you that.'

She swallowed, her eyes still on the rail.

Stores brought the clothes to him?

Noticing a selection of expensive cosmetics laid out on a nearby table, she blinked in amazement. It seemed that nothing had been left to chance.

She strolled over to the rail, trying to look as though this sort of thing happened to her every day. She'd never had the opportunity to even look at clothes of this quality and style before, let alone wear them. In awe she fingered a silk skirt so short that it was almost indecent.

'Good choice,' he said cynically from immediately behind her. 'That skirt has ''slut'' written all over it, and seeing as that's what you are you might as well advertise the fact.'

She turned on him, eyes flashing with hurt, her blonde hair

tumbling over her shoulders. 'And if I'm a slut, what does that make you?'

'Sexually satisfied,' he mocked, removing her towel with a single, purposeful jerk of his bronzed hand.

She gave a gasp of shock and grabbed at the towel but he held it out of reach, his eyes slightly narrowed as they swept over her naked body.

'You really do have the most amazing body,' he murmured, skimming a hand over one full breast. Immediately Alesia's nipples peaked and he gave a low laugh. 'And you really, *really* want me, don't you? If we weren't pushed for time I'd take you straight back to bed and try yet another position.'

Her face scarlet with mortification, Alesia tried to turn away from him but he swung her round to face him, his hands holding her firmly.

'Just don't be tempted to flirt with anyone else tonight,' he warned. 'You may be a slut but you're mine alone. I *never* share.'

Flirt?

Still horribly conscious of her nudity, Alesia stared at him in disbelief, reminding herself that this man knew absolutely *nothing* about her. She'd never flirted in her life and wouldn't even know where to begin. Because of her situation she'd always avoided that sort of contact with men. Had avoided relationships deeper than friendship.

Sebastien reached out a hand and grabbed a top from the rail. 'Wear this with the skirt,' he ordered, 'and no bra.'

She stared at the clothes in dismay. She'd never worn anything like them in her life. 'I c-can't go braless,' she stammered. 'I'm too—'

'Curvaceous?' he taunted her. 'Plenty of people out there are wondering why I married you. I intend to show them.'

Goaded beyond reason by his taunts, she turned on him. 'Are you sure you wouldn't prefer me to just go out in my underwear?' Her tone dripped sarcasm and he gave a slow smile.

'This is going to be even sexier than underwear, trust me.'

Alesia closed her eyes. She couldn't believe this was happening. 'You can't make me wear that outfit.'

'Don't test me, Alesia,' he warned softly.

'Fine.' She yanked the outfit out of his hand, grabbed a handful of the cosmetics and shot him a defiant look. 'If you want the whole world to know you married a slut, then that's up to you. Let's broadcast it, shall we?'

She stalked into the bathroom and slammed the door behind her.

CHAPTER SIX

SEBASTIEN checked his watch and paced the length of his bedroom one more time.

Never before had he had reason to question his mental acuity, but nothing about his new wife was making sense. She was an heiress in her own right, had demanded an extortionate sum of money from him on his wedding day, *a sum which he knew had already vanished from her account*—and yet there were no visible signs of profligate spending. She'd led a pampered and privileged existence from the day she was born, and yet she'd been in the kitchen making her own lunch as if she did it every day. And she'd been wearing a pair of ancient jeans that no previous woman of his acquaintance would have been seen dead in. It did not add up.

When he'd married Alesia Philipos he'd expected rich, pampered, shallow and boring. In his eyes her only redeeming feature had been her incredible face and body and her apparent willingness to display it. What he *hadn't* expected was complex—and his new wife was definitely complex.

Realising that she'd been in the bathroom for the best part of an hour, Sebastien stared at the closed door in brooding contemplation. What could she be doing in there that was taking so long?

Never good at waiting at the best of times, he was at the point of breaking down the bathroom door in search of an answer when the lock finally clicked and Alesia stepped back into the bedroom.

Sebastien stilled, his usually restless gaze arrested by the girl standing in front of him.

Only years of experience in controlling his facial expression prevented his jaw from hitting the ground.

Whatever she'd been doing in the bathroom all that time, the end result was spectacular.

She was drop dead gorgeous. Beautiful.

Her skin was pale and flawless, the faint brush of colour on her cheeks simply emphasizing the perfect shape of her face. Her incredible violet eyes looked larger than ever and the subtle sheen of colour applied to her lips simply accentuated the tempting curve of her mouth.

Sebastian bit back a groan of lust as his eyes raked every delectable inch of her in unashamed masculine appreciation.

She shouldn't have looked like that in the outfit he'd chosen.

She should have looked like a cheap tart. Instead she managed to look innocent and seductively feminine at the same time, although how a woman could contrive to look innocent in a skirt barely wider than a belt, he couldn't imagine. Her slender legs went on for ever, the miniskirt skimmed her perfectly shaped bottom and the tiny top exposed a tantalizing stretch of feminine midriff. It was just tight enough to offer support to her full breasts and Sebastien's body hardened in urgent and immediate response. For a brief but distinctly unsettling moment he struggled to remember why they had to leave the bedroom.

It was just as well he had a reliable team of bodyguards, he reflected grimly as he wrestled his emotions under control, because otherwise he'd have trouble keeping people away from her. *Men* away from her.

Sebastien ground his teeth, astonished by how possessive he felt over a woman he didn't even like.

'You insisted on this outfit so you can stop staring,' she said stiffly, 'and I probably ought to warn you that I'm not used to walking in heels this high, so unless you want me to break an ankle I'm gong to have to hold your arm.'

Taken aback by her candid admission that she'd rarely worn heels before and mentally adding that muttered confession to a growing list of facts that just didn't add up, Sebastien frowned as he felt her hand slide over his biceps.

'It's hold you or fall over. Otherwise, believe me, I wouldn't touch you with a bargepole. I hope you're well insured,' she muttered, stooping with a pained frown and sliding a finger along the strap. 'If I tread on anyone's foot while I'm dancing in these I'm going to cause *serious* damage.'

He gritted his teeth and refrained from pointing out that she wouldn't be dancing with anyone but him. Not given to making mistakes, Sebastien was forced to admit that in this case he'd made a serious error of judgement.

He'd intended her to dress like a tart to remind him of the woman she really was, because he was finding those huge eyes and that innocent expression profoundly distracting. Instead he'd turned her into nothing short of a walking temptation.

Staring down into her beautiful face, he suddenly realized that the glow of almost childlike innocence came from inside her. Nothing she wore would ever make her look cheap because she just exuded class.

A well-disguised gold-digger, he reminded himself grimly, reaching for his jacket and striding towards the door.

No matter how stunning she was or how exciting his new wife was in bed, there was no way that he'd be forgetting what had brought her there in the first place.

His money.

In the back of the limousine Alesia felt the slide of expensive leather under her bare thighs and stared down at her glamorously shod feet with almost childish fascination. A bubble of laughter threatened to erupt inside her and she struggled to hold it back. She just *loved* the shoes. They were sexy and glamorous and totally frivolous and she'd never owned anything frivolous before in her life. *And she loved the clothes.* And the make-up. She'd never had the money to spend on cosmetics before so she had absolutely no experience of applying them, which was why she'd taken so long in the bathroom.

After the first effort she'd looked like a clown, and after the second she'd managed to look as though she had a cold. Finally, after her face had been given time to settle down from all the washing and scrubbing, she'd managed to master the art of subtle enhancement and she'd been delighted with the result. And, although she felt hideously self-conscious in such revealing clothes, she also felt beautiful. Was this what it was like to be seriously rich? She wrapped one long leg over the other and felt a flash of satisfaction as she saw Sebastien's molten gaze settle on the length of thigh exposed by the ridiculous skirt.

He wanted her.

She resisted the temptation to smile and smile. He might loathe and despise her but he *definitely* wanted her. And he might pretend to be ultra cool about it, but surely no man could spend six hours in bed with a woman if he were as bored and indifferent as he pretended to be?

Lost in her own private thoughts, a sudden flash of light in her face made her jump and she gave a gasp and shrank back in her seat while Sebastien gave a soft curse.

'Paparazzi,' he muttered by way of explanation as the car slid to a halt outside a glitzy-looking building. 'They won't be allowed in the club so just smile and don't speak.'

'What is it about Greek men that keeps them well and truly stuck in the Stone Age? I'm *always* being told not to speak.' Alesia reached for her bag, hoping that she could manage to walk as far as the door of the nightclub without twisting her ankle. 'Someone ought to tell you that these days women are supposed to have a voice.'

Sebastien caught her arm and prevented her from leaving the car. 'Carlo will open the door. It prevents the press getting too close,' he said smoothly. 'And, for your information, I have a totally modern outlook when it comes to the role of women. You can speak whenever you choose. But not to the press.'

Totally modern?

Alesia gaped at him, wondering if he truly knew himself at all. This was a man who told her how to wear her hair and how to dress and who clearly saw her prime role as being to satisfy his rampant sexual needs. And he thought he was modern?

Before she could enlighten him as to the true meaning of the word, the car door opened and she was ushered into the nightclub amidst an explosion of flashbulbs and photographers yelling for her to look this way and that.

One photographer came in too close and was instantly blocked by two of Sebastien's security team.

Alesia glanced around her in confusion and astonishment. 'I can't think why they're suddenly so interested in me,' she muttered and Sebastien flashed her a seductive smile that seriously threatened her ability to walk in a straight line.

'Because I married you, *agape mou*,' he drawled lazily, 'and our two families have been at war for three generations. Newspaper editors the world over are loving it and so are the gossip magazines. Photographs of us will sell for a small fortune.'

People would *pay* for photographs of them?

Why? She was just an ordinary girl dressed up in designer clothes!

Casting a shimmering glance in her direction, Sebastien lifted an eyebrow. '*How* did your grandfather manage to keep you hidden from the media for all those years, tell me that?'

Alesia dragged her fascinated gaze away from the banks of photographers jolting for her attention. 'I—er—I led a very private life,' she muttered vaguely, wondering again why anyone would be remotely interested in staring at a photograph of her. The outfit was nice, but still...

Alesia allowed herself to be ushered into the sleek, ultra-modern club and gazed around in awe. The club was crowded with beautiful people and she realized suddenly that her impossibly tiny skirt didn't look remotely out of place in this setting.

'This place is crowded with people wearing nothing but underwear.' She raised her voice to be heard above the music and Sebastien raised a dark eyebrow in response to her comment and then gave a reluctant smile.

'Dancing is hot work.'

Watching the gyrations on the dance floor, Alesia opened her mouth to confess that she'd never been to a nightclub in her life before and then realized that such a confession would betray far too much about her.

Evidently he believed her to be a real party animal: a rich, pampered heiress who spent her entire life shopping and then modelling the results. This was supposed to be her natural habitat.

She stared around in fascination, drinking it all in. She'd never been *anywhere* like this.

Coloured lights swirled and flashed, various effects shimmered and smoked and through it all the pounding, pulsing beat of the music tempted more and more people on to the exotically lit dance floor.

Alesia felt a thrill of excitement that she couldn't quite identify. Suddenly, more than anything, she wanted to be on that dance floor. She wanted to let her body move to the compelling, hypnotic rhythm. *She wanted to enjoy herself.*

She turned to Sebastien, her eyes bright and her lips parted. 'I want to dance.'

And dance and dance...

Night-black eyes clashed with hers and his hard mouth lifted in mockery. 'With or without the shoes?'

She didn't care. She just wanted to *move*.

'I'll start with shoes and then we'll see—' Aware that they were still attracting a significant degree of interest, she glanced around with a frown. 'Do people *never* stop staring?'

'You are the granddaughter of one of the richest men in the world,' he drawled, casting a cynical glance over his broad shoulder. 'Like me, you must be used to it. People always stare. You know that.'

She bit her lip and tried to look casual and confident, as though being the object of everyone's attention was an everyday occurrence.

With an air of bored cool that reflected his total lack of interest in the people gawping at them, Sebastien threaded his fingers through hers and led her on to the dance floor, retaining his possessive grip on her as they moved together.

The music pounded and pulsed and Alesia closed her eyes and discovered for the first time in her life that she just *loved* to dance. She loved the silken brush of her hair as it swished from side to side, loved the sinuous sway of her body as she moved her hips and arms to the addictive rhythm of the music. In fact she loved it *all*.

She danced to record after record, her body seduced by the hectic rhythm of the music and the relative anonymity of the crowded dance floor.

Finally the music slowed and Sebastien hauled her against him in a characteristically possessive gesture which should have annoyed her but for some reason made her already wide smile widen even further.

He was easily the best-looking guy in the room and all the women were staring at him. And she was willing to bet that they would have been staring even if he hadn't been rich and famous and useful for selling newspapers to a public hungry for a diet of celebrity gossip. Sebastien Fiorukis was a man who would stand out in the densest crowd. It was like parking a sleek Ferrari in a bicycle shed. He just looked *expensive* and he had an air of power and command that would always draw women like moths to a bright flame.

But for tonight he was with *her*, she thought, gleeful as a child as she intercepted the envious glances cast in her direction.

Trying to see him as a stranger would, her eyes skimmed over his glossy dark hair and slid to the hint of bronzed skin visible at the neck of his shirt. He looked every inch the multi-millionaire that he was. Vibrant, driven and successful at everything he touched. A man who didn't know the meaning of the word failure. He was part of her new costume and every bit as glamorous and sophisticated as the shoes and the designer outfit.

They danced until her feet ached and her throat was parched and finally she agreed to his suggestion that they break for a drink.

Responding to an impulse that she didn't understand, she wound her arms around him and gave him a spontaneous hug before they left the dance floor. 'Oh, Sebastien, thank you.' Breathless and laughing, her eyes shone as she looked up at him. 'This is fantastic and I'm having the *best* time—' She felt him stiffen and watched as stunned dark eyes swept her flushed cheeks.

'You're behaving as though you've never been to a night-club before.'

'I haven't. I mean, not one like this,' she corrected herself quickly, wincing at her own mistake. Aware that he was studying her with a curious expression on his face, she tilted her head questioningly, still breathless from wild dancing, her eyes shining with an excitement that she couldn't even begin to conceal.

She knew she should be playing it cool, looking bored and indifferent as if she spent her life in places like this, but she just couldn't. There was too much adrenalin flowing through her veins, too much excitement—

In fact, she wanted the evening never to end—

'What?' She tried to slow her breathing. 'You're staring at me because I've got a red face, aren't you?'

His eyes narrowed. 'I'm staring at you because I've never seen you smile before.'

'Well, I'm having a nice time.' Forgetting to be guarded, she glanced back at the dance floor regretfully. 'Do you think we could—'

'No,' Sebastian drawled immediately, taking her hand and leading her to a vacant table with a prime view of the dance floor. 'We definitely couldn't. I'm a man in need of a drink.'

Alesia registered that her shoes were digging into her feet and plopped gratefully on to one of the chairs, wondering why this table was free when the rest of the club was heaving with people. She felt tired and just *ridiculously* happy. She was uncovering a whole new side to herself that she'd never even known existed. She'd always assumed that she wasn't like other girls. That she didn't enjoy partying, clothes or other 'girly' pursuits. But now she realized that she'd never actually been given a chance to experience those things. And the truth was she loved them. For the first time in her life she could be self-indulgent and just *enjoy* herself.

She was just wondering at exactly what point she dared suggest venturing back on the dance floor when the crowds pressing in on their table parted.

'Sebastien! You came!' A tall, slender woman wearing an indecently low-cut black dress shimmered up to their table, her glossy mouth curved into a predatory smile. 'I'm *so* pleased.'

'Ariadne.' Sebastien rose to his feet and kissed the woman on both cheeks. 'You've surpassed yourself. I predict a massive success.'

The woman threw a satisfied glance at the heaving dance

floor. 'Captivating, isn't it? And stylish. We're already having to restrict membership.' Her slim fingers curled possessively over his forearm, the scarlet nails gleaming like a warning. 'I'm glad you came. I reserved you the best table.'

Sebastien's gaze fastened on those reddened lips and he smiled. 'Thanks.'

'I *really* need the benefit of your business brain.' Ariadne slid into the vacant seat next to him, not glancing once in Alesia's direction. 'We've come up against a couple of problems and I might need you to use your influence—' Ariadne's voice lowered and she leaned closer to Sebastien, her hand snaking around his strong neck, drawing his head towards her reddened lips ostensibly so that she could keep the conversation private.

Watching this interaction with frowning dismay, Alesia felt her newly discovered happiness drain out of her. It was quite clear that his relationship with this woman was far more intimate than simple friendship. Was she one of his mistresses? And, if so, past or current? The thought that he'd shared with other women what he'd shared with her made her feel physically ill. If she needed any more evidence that to him it was just sex then she had it now.

And, to make matters worse, the woman hadn't even glanced in her direction. It was as if she didn't exist.

Feeling as miserable as she had been happy only moments earlier, Alesia reached for the drink that had been placed by her hand and took several large mouthfuls.

She sat and drank, waiting to be included in the conversation, waiting for Sebastien to introduce her, but he lounged easily in the chair, his handsome face giving nothing away as he listened attentively to the woman who was all but wrapped around him in an attempt to exclude Alesia.

She couldn't help being aware of the curious stares being cast in her direction. It was hardly surprising that people were looking, she thought gloomily. They were supposed to be newly married and yet Sebastien had clearly forgotten her existence.

Ignored and abandoned, Alesia felt her temper begin to rise as she finished her drink.

Why should she sit there pretending to be invisible?

Too disgusted to watch them any longer and feeling unaccountably light-headed, she fixed her gaze back on the dance floor, feeling a stab of envy as she watched the dancing. On the dance floor she'd had fun. She'd lost herself in the moment. So why shouldn't she do so again? She held her breath, checking out the number of women dancing alone. There were plenty.

So why shouldn't she join them?

Without so much as a glance towards her companions, Alesia lifted her chin and stood up, clutching at the table for a moment to gain her balance and then walking purposefully on to the dance floor, looking neither left or right. If anyone was staring, she didn't want to know.

Once again the music slid into her soul and she closed her eyes and tipped her head back, feeling the rhythm flow over her and letting her body move in time. She spun and gyrated, her hair flying across her face, her arms above her head, her hips swaying.

After several minutes a tall blonde man joined her and it was so much fun to be dancing with someone again that she just smiled and matched her movements to his. Nothing mattered, she thought happily, except having fun *right now*.

She lowered her eyelashes in mute invitation, spun closer and then felt hard fingers digging into her shoulder, hauling her back in a gesture of pure masculine possession. Caught off balance, she staggered and would have collapsed in a heap had not she been held firmly against rock-solid muscle. Dizzily she glanced upwards and clashed with stormy dark eyes shimmering with barely restrained anger. Keeping her clamped against him in an iron grip, Sebastien spoke in

Greek to her dance partner and, although Alesia didn't understand a word of what he said, there was no misunderstanding his icy tone or the barely veiled threat in those midnight-black eyes. She frowned as the blond man cast a nervous glance at the width of Sebastien's shoulders and melted back into the crowd.

'What a wimp—' Alesia muttered with disdain. 'He might at least have stayed to finish the dance.'

'He had more sense,' Sebastien observed harshly, all the volatility of his Mediterranean heritage revealed in his glittering dark gaze. 'Which is more than can be said for you. We are in a public place and you are *not* supposed to be part of the entertainment. If you want to dance then you dance with me.'

She glared at him and tried to pull away. 'You were busy.'

'Then you should have waited.'

'For what? For you to decide you'd had enough of *that woman*?'

His eyes narrowed. '*That woman* happens to be the owner of this club. She is the reason we came here tonight. She needed my advice.'

'*Don't* treat me as if I'm stupid,' Alesia advised hotly, stabbing a finger into his broad chest. 'She was all over you like wrapping paper. And if *you're* going to seduce other women in public then *I'll* dance with who I like.'

Sebastien's hand curled over hers. Every inch of her body was locked against his and the feel of his hard, muscular frame made her head spin with longing.

Oh, help—

'Flirt again,' he warned, his tone lethally soft, 'and you'll discover *exactly* what it's like to be married to a Greek man.'

Heart thumping, knees shaking, Alesia stared at him helplessly and gave a tiny moan of self-disgust. How could she find this man so attractive? Trying to halt the insidious warmth that was spreading through her body, she made an attempt to pull away but he simply tightened his grip. Reminding herself that he'd just spent the best part of the evening stuck to another woman, Alesia gritted her teeth. 'I already know what it's like to be married to a Greek man, Sebastien. It's lonely and frustrating. You marry me, then you vanish for two weeks without telling me where you're going and then you take me out for an evening and proceed to flirt with someone else. I *hate* you.'

And what she hated most was the fact that she *cared*.

Colour streaked his magnificent cheekbones. 'I was not "flirting".'

'You were,' Alesia informed him unsteadily. 'Your eyes were all over her and she couldn't stop touching you and you forgot I was even there. Well, I refuse to be ignored! You chose to bring me here and then you were *rude*. And, what's more, everyone was watching.' Suddenly she felt horribly dizzy and clutched at him for support. 'And now I feel a bit sick.'

The breath hissed through his teeth and he muttered under his breath. 'Have you been drinking?'

She frowned, wondering why her head was swimming. 'I never drink.'

His mouth tightened. 'You downed most of your drink in one mouthful.'

'I was thirsty.'

'Then you should have drunk water,' he suggested helpfully, holding her firmly when her legs would have given way. 'For the record, alcohol is not the best thirst quencher.'

She leaned her forehead against his chest and wished the room would stop spinning. 'All I've drunk is the lemonade you gave me. I've probably just been twirled around too many times. That man was a very good dancer.'

'The drink was vodka with a dash of lemonade,' he said grimly, 'and I think you're not safe to be left for five minutes unattended. You're like a child at its first party.'

'And you're horrible,' she muttered, lifting her face to his, struggling to focus as she tried to remember exactly what it was that she hated about him. 'You do all those things to me in bed and then you just walk out and never say *anything* nice. Not one single thing. I just don't understand why women think you're so amazing. You don't make sense and I can't keep up with you. And I don't think I can pretend to be the person you think I am any more. It's just *exhausting*.'

Sebastien stilled, every muscle in his powerful body suddenly tense as he focused all his attention on her. 'Run that past me again?'

There was something in his tone that rang alarm bells but her head was too fuzzy to work it all out. 'You never say anything nice to me when we're in bed—'

'Not that bit—the other bit.' Thick dark lashes swooped downwards, concealing his expression. 'The bit about not being able to pretend any more.'

'Well, I'm not this stupid, brainless heiress and frankly it's a struggle to pretend that I am,' she muttered. 'I've never worn a designer dress in my life, I've never had time to party and you think I'm some sort of *mammoth* slut and yet I've never even—' She broke off and he raised a dark eyebrow in question.

'Yes?' he prompted her helpfully, his dark gaze still fixed on her face. 'Never even—?'

The loosening effects of the drink were fading and she was suddenly swamped by a horrid, horrid feeling that she'd just said totally the wrong thing but she couldn't exactly work out what. Suddenly all she wanted to do was sleep.

'Well, I'm not a slut,' she repeated vaguely, 'although I like the clothes they wear. Except the shoes hurt.'

Her head thudded back against his chest and she heard him swear softly and then felt him scoop her into his arms.

She wanted to tell him that he had to get out of the habit of carrying her everywhere but it felt so nice being back in his arms that she just gave a sigh and nestled her head into his shoulder.

'You smell *so* good,' she muttered dreamily, 'but I'm absolutely *not* getting back into bed with you until you learn to say something *nice*. It makes me feel horrid.'

He didn't answer but she saw his jaw tighten and felt him lengthen his stride.

Cool air brushed her bare legs as he emerged from the nightclub and seconds later he deposited her on the back seat of the limo before leaning forward and hitting a button. He delivered a set of instructions to his driver in terse, clipped Greek and then sank back against the seat with a grim expression on his handsome face.

Alesia curled up on the seat like a baby and struggled not to be sick. 'I'm never dancing again,' she groaned, closing her eyes and then opening them again quickly as the dizziness intensified. 'The whole world is still spinning.'

'That's the alcohol, *not* the dancing,' he informed her, shooting her a glance of naked exasperation, 'and I can't *believe* you've reached the age of twenty-two without knowing how it feels to get drunk.'

'I've reached the age of twenty-two without knowing how a lot of things feel,' she confessed sleepily, her words slurring as her head dropped back against the leather seat. 'These last few weeks have been one long new experience for me. Some of them good, some of them not so good. The worst by far was when you—'

'—didn't say anything nice to you in bed,' he finished for her, inhaling deeply like a man at the extreme limits of his patience. 'You've already told me that several times. I get the message.'

Alesia shifted her head slightly so that she could focus on him. 'Actually, I was going to say when you flirted with another woman in front of me,' she murmured, studying the harsh lines of his bronzed face and deciding that he really was shockingly handsome. 'As new experiences go, that really was the pits. But I love the clothes and the shoes. And dancing was amazing. I want you to take me again. Maybe tomorrow.'

He studied her through narrowed dark eyes, his gaze suddenly disturbingly intent. 'Tomorrow,' he warned in a soft voice, 'I have other plans for you.'

Alesia groaned. At the moment she just wanted to be left to sleep. 'Well, I expect you will have done one of your vanishing acts again by the morning,' she muttered hopefully as her eyes drifted shut again.

'No chance,' Sebastien murmured, leaning across to catch her before she sprawled on to the seat. 'I'm going to start getting to the bottom of the person you really are, *agape mou*. Tomorrow, you and I are going to start really getting to know each other.'

Alesia woke with a pounding headache.

'Drink this.' The deep, masculine drawl came from right beside her and she groaned and kept her eyes firmly closed.

'I can't drink anything—'

'It will help.' He slid an arm under her shoulders, lifted her as if she weighed nothing and put the glass to her lips.

Alesia took a tentative sip and wrinkled her nose. 'It tastes disgusting.'

'Then maybe your education regarding the effects of alcohol is truly complete,' he said drily. 'Trust me, it will help.'

She sipped from the glass, froze for a moment while her churning stomach protested and then relaxed. 'You're right. I feel better.'

'Good. Because you have less than an hour to get ready.' He straightened and she realized that he was already showered and dressed.

She stared at him in disbelief. 'Not more nightclubs.'

'It's lunchtime,' he informed her helpfully, gesturing towards the window with a sweep of his bronzed hand, 'so no, not more nightclubs. They don't generally open until midnight but you wouldn't know that, would you, given that you'd never been to one before?'

There was something in his silky tone that smelt of danger and she looked at him anxiously. Much of the previous night was a blur. Had she really told him that? 'I—er—' She cleared her throat awkwardly as she tried to work out how to rescue herself from the current situation. 'I didn't exactly say I hadn't been in a nightclub.'

'Yes, you did. Along with a great number of other fascinating revelations which I can't wait to explore in greater detail.' Sebastien glanced at his watch and then strode towards the door. 'I have some important calls to make before we leave, so take advantage of the time to have a shower but don't fall asleep again. My pilot will pick us up in less than an hour.'

The sickness returned. 'Your pilot?'

'That's right.' He opened the door and glanced back at her. 'We're going on our honeymoon. Better late than never, as the saying goes.'

'Honeymoon?' She gaped at him. 'But we weren't going to have a honeymoon. You said you didn't want to spend that much time with me.'

'That was because I thought one night with you would be enough. I was wrong. I've tried cold water and I've tried avoiding you,' he told her frankly. 'Nothing works. So we'll try a different approach.'

Her mouth fell open. 'You tried avoiding me? That's why you vanished for two weeks? You were avoiding me?'

'Yes, but it didn't work. I've accepted the way things are. We're married. It's perfectly acceptable for us to spend time together and I need to get you out of my system if I'm ever to stand a chance of concentrating again.'

She stared at him, feeling slightly faint. 'And how do you propose to do that?'

'By having endless, uninterrupted sex, *agape mou*.' He flashed her a smile. 'In less than an hour it will be just you and I and a very private island. You won't even have to dress in underwear—so don't bother to pack.'

CHAPTER SEVEN

THEY were flying over the sea again.

Was Greece nothing but ocean?

Alesia closed her eyes and tried to visualize land. Tried to control the almost frantic panic that erupted inside her.

'You can open your eyes,' Sebastien said, his voice tinged with amusement as he lounged in the seat next to her. 'We land in less than five minutes and you're missing the best view in Greece.'

Alesia kept her eyes shut. She wasn't interested in the view. She was thinking about the water. Fathoms and fathoms of ocean laid out beneath her just waiting to claim the unwary—

'*Theos mou*, you are white as a sheet.' His voice was suddenly sharp with concern. 'Is this still a consequence of last night?'

She couldn't speak, fighting her own private battle against the terror that threatened to engulf her.

There was a moment's silence and then strong fingers wrapped themselves around her cold hand. 'I remember now that you were the same colour the first time I met you. I didn't know you were so afraid of flying,' he said quietly. 'Forgive me. Next time we use the boat. It makes the journey a little longer but at least it will be more comfortable for you.'

At that her eyes flew open in shock. The fact that he seemed to care whether or not she liked the helicopter surprised her.

Why would he care?

Perhaps he was just afraid that she might be ill. Didn't

men hate it when women were ill? Should she confess that it was the water, not the flying?

That a boat would be even worse.

'There's no need to look at me like that,' he drawled softly. 'Everyone has a weakness. It's almost a relief to know that you have something other than just greed. You can relax now. We've landed. Welcome to my private hideaway.'

Remembering how close the helicopter pad was to the sea from their first meeting, Alesia was tempted to shut her eyes again but she forced them to stay open, knowing that she somehow had to get herself to the villa.

The sea wasn't going to leap up and grab her, she reminded herself firmly as she descended quickly and stood on the Tarmac. This fear of hers was totally irrational and it was time she tried to conquer it.

'You are still very pale.' Sebastien surveyed her with frowning contemplation and then spoke several words in Greek to his pilot, who melted into the background. 'You should lie down before dinner. Or perhaps you would prefer a swim?'

Should she confess that she never swam?

Should she tell him—?

She licked dry lips, her heart suddenly racing with fear. 'Maybe later.'

'After a few days in Athens most people can't wait to dive into the ocean,' he said, amusement flickering in his dark eyes as he glanced in her direction. 'But there's plenty of time. I have no plans to rush back to the city.'

Alesia hid her dismay.

How long exactly was he planning on staying?

It would be harder for her to phone her mother from here and if she didn't receive a call, she'd worry.

Sebastien frowned. 'You are unbelievably tense and the whole point of this trip is for you to unwind. There is nothing to do here but relax. You must still be tired after last night.'

He sounded as if he cared that she was tired and she stared at him in confusion. Why was he being nice to her all of a sudden?

Alesia gave a stiff smile. 'I am tired, you're right.'

'Have a lie down before dinner—'

They walked into the villa and Alesia's eyes widened as she glanced around her. When they'd visited the island for that first meeting, she hadn't actually set foot inside the house itself.

The living area was huge and light, decorated in blues and whites with acres of cool creamy marble. Exotic plants nestled in the corner of the room and on the walls hung several huge, brightly coloured canvases. 'It's *beautiful*—'

'My cousin designed it,' he told her, pausing by her side. 'She has her own interior design business. She is responsible for the paintings as well.'

'She's very talented,' Alesia breathed and then her eye settled on the grand piano in the corner of the room and she gave a gasp of pleasure and surprise. 'Oh!'

He followed the direction of her gaze with a quizzical frown. 'You play?'

Alesia hurried over to the piano and ran a hand lovingly over the wood. 'Yes.'

His eyes narrowed and he gestured towards the piano. 'Be my guest.'

She flushed and shook her head. 'No—it's fine. I don't— well—'

'You don't what?' His voice was soft. 'You don't want to tell me that much about yourself? Was that what your grandfather told you, Alesia? To hide the person you really are?'

Her gaze flew to his and she stared at him in consternation. 'I—'

'We're married now, *agape mou*,' he said calmly. 'The deal is signed and sealed. Nothing you do or say can change that. It's time to relax and be yourself.'

'I am myself.'

He gave a wry smile. 'No. You're back to being the zipped-up version of yourself. Last night, I suspect, I had a glimpse of the real person.'

Dismay flickered through her. 'I had too much to drink—'

'And clearly that lowered your inhibitions sufficiently for you to reveal your true self,' he drawled, dark eyes glittering as he surveyed her with no small degree of amusement. 'I discovered last night that my little kitten has claws.'

She flushed and bit her lip. 'You upset me—'

'A lapse that won't occur again,' he slotted in smoothly, reaching out a hand and pulling her towards him. 'I discovered that my wife has a personality which I suspect she obediently buried on the orders of her grandfather.'

Alesia swallowed. 'I—'

'From now on I want you to be yourself,' he commanded, sliding a strong hand around her waist and pulling her against him. 'I want to know everything about you. No secrets.'

No secrets.

Alesia closed her eyes. He still believed that her mother was dead, killed alongside her father. But to have told him the truth would have revealed that her grandfather *hated* her and that this marriage had nothing to do with mending fences and everything to do with revenge.

If he discovered the extent of her deception—if he discovered *everything*—then there would be no containing his anger—

At some point he was bound to find out and the thought of his reaction just sickened her.

'I need to lie down—'

Sebastien muttered something under his breath in Greek. 'You are never touching alcohol again,' he vowed, taking her hand and leading her through to the master-bedroom suite.

Like the rest of the villa it was an elegant and simply

decorated room and Alesia glanced around and then looked through the open glass doors on to the shady vine-covered terrace and beyond that to the large swimming pool. 'It's amazing.'

Apart from the pool, of course, but she intended to ignore that.

Suddenly she realized that the villa was a home in the way that his Athenian mansion never could be. It was full of personal touches that revealed secrets about the owner. And it was wonderfully private and quiet.

Quiet.

'Where is everyone?'

He frowned. 'Everyone?'

She waved a hand. 'Usually you are surrounded by staff—'

He gave a wry smile. 'This is my retreat. My private bolthole. I don't think it would fit into that category if I filled it full of staff, do you? This is the place I come to forget my responsibilities as an employer.'

She stared at him. 'We're on our own here? Just us?'

'Just us.' His voice was velvety smooth and she felt her heart miss a beat.

Suddenly she was aware of every vibrant, masculine inch of him.

Reminding herself that only last night he'd been wrapped around another woman, she lifted her chin and met his eyes with a challenging gaze.

'So who cooks, Sebastien?'

'We share it,' he said smoothly, his glance not flickering from her face. 'A boat delivers fresh produce on a daily basis. Discovering what is in the parcel is half the fun.'

Her mouth fell open. 'You cook? But Greek men never cook—'

Her grandfather didn't so much as make a cup of coffee.

'I frequently come here alone,' he told her calmly, 'so it was learn to cook or starve.'

Alesia stared at him in confusion, realizing that perhaps she didn't know him as well as she thought she did. But just exactly how much time had she spent with her new husband? she reminded herself. Virtually none. Apart from their wedding day, when they had barely been on speaking terms, the only time they'd spent together up until the nightclub had been spent in bed. They hadn't even shared a meal since their wedding.

Sebastien walked over to the glass doors and slid them open. 'Lie down for a few hours. I'll be on the terrace if you need anything.'

Alesia waited for him to go and then stripped down to her underwear and slid between the cool sheets with a sigh of relief.

Her head was still pounding from lack of sleep and the alcohol she'd unwittingly consumed the night before and suddenly nothing seemed clear any more.

Telling herself that she'd work it all out later, she drifted into a deep sleep.

When she awoke it was sunset and she sat up feeling guilty. How long had she slept? Too long—

And there was no sign of Sebastien.

She slid out of bed and searched for her jeans.

'They have been disposed of,' came a dark drawl from the doorway and she gave a start and shot back into bed, pulling the sheet up to her neck.

'You scared me—'

He surveyed her with no small degree of amusement. 'Since we are the only two people on the island, I couldn't have been anyone else. And your schoolgirl modesty is totally unnecessary, *agape mou*. I'm perfectly happy for you to walk around naked.'

She flushed to the roots of her hair. 'Well, I'm *not* happy,' she muttered, wondering if she'd ever feel comfortable with her body in the way that he did. 'And what do you mean, you've disposed of my jeans? You told me not to pack anything. The only clothes I have are the ones I was wearing earlier.'

'And you won't be wearing them again,' he said smoothly, strolling into the room. He'd changed into a pair of cool linen trousers, the sleeves of his casual shirt rolled up to reveal bronzed forearms dusted with dark hairs. 'Since you didn't appear to have purchased anything suitable for a hot climate, I took the liberty of arranging a suitable wardrobe for you.'

Still clutching the sheet, she gazed at him warily. 'A wardrobe?'

He knew she hadn't bought anything. He knew—

She closed her eyes. Well, of course he knew. He'd been into her dressing room in Athens and seen it empty apart from her wedding dress, her jeans and a few tops and, whatever else he might be, the man wasn't stupid.

'You're not used to shopping, are you?' His tone conversational, he walked into her dressing room and returned carrying a narrow sheath of peacock-blue silk. 'An intriguing quality in someone who clearly requires such a large income to support her lifestyle.'

Alesia froze and waited in horrified stillness for him to ask the obvious question—*why* she'd demanded so much money when she didn't even seem to spend it.

Frantically rummaging around in her brain for a suitable answer and coming up with none, she almost cried with relief when he simply dropped the dress in her lap.

'Get dressed,' he ordered quietly, strolling back towards the terrace with a thoughtful glance in her direction, 'and then meet me on the terrace. We'll have supper and talk.'

Talk?

Alesia fingered the beautiful dress and stared after him in dismay. It had been easier when Sebastien had done his vanishing act, she conceded. At least then she hadn't had to worry about giving anything away.

Suddenly he seemed to have developed a desire to get to know her and that was going to present her with a big problem.

Fresh from the discovery that his new wife was certainly *not* lacking in personality, Sebastien lounged on the sun-baked terrace, staring at the azure-blue pool in brooding contemplation.

Never before had he felt confused by a woman. Out of control.

In his experience their behaviour followed a totally predictable pattern. They shopped, they lunched, they partied. Even when he switched one woman for another, which he did with monotonous regularity, the pattern didn't change.

So he'd never had any expectations that his new wife would prove to be different. Hadn't she, sole heiress to the Philipos fortune, demanded an enormous sum of money to marry him?

Once in possession of such generous funds, he'd expected her to shop and shop until her feet were blistered and yet it was rapidly becoming clear to him that she hadn't purchased a single item of clothing since their wedding day.

And maybe not before then, either.

When confronted with a selection of exclusive designer outfits, she didn't behave like any woman he'd ever met before.

In fact, her frank delight at the clothes he'd produced for her trip to the nightclub suggested that she'd virtually never purchased an item of clothing in her life.

As a male with endless experience in the art of pleasing the opposite sex, Sebastien had been forced to endure countless shopping sessions with women who contrived to look suitably bored by the whole procedure. Never had he known a woman to display such undisguised enthusiasm for clothes. Alesia had behaved like a child who'd just discovered the fun of dressing up.

Which left him with the intriguing and puzzling question of just *how* she'd spent his money. And he knew that she *had* spent it because her account was empty, but so far no one had been able to give him an answer to the question of exactly where the money had gone.

None of it made sense. And neither did his own reaction to her.

He gave a soft curse as hot molten lust thudded through him and the force of his own hunger once more threatened to overwhelm him. *Never* before had he felt this out of control around a woman. Only moments ago he'd been forced to leave the room because the sight of her lying there, sleepy-eyed and pink-cheeked, had made him want to pin her to the bed and keep her horizontal using the most basic and satisfying method known to man.

Even six hours in bed with her the previous afternoon hadn't cooled his ravenous libido. He'd had no intention of patronizing the opening of Ariadne's nightclub but he'd needed to do something to take his mind off his mounting sexual hunger for his new bride.

For a man whose attention span with women had always been alarmingly short, his reaction was as mystifying as it was frustrating and it didn't help to acknowledge that seeing her dancing with another man had forced him to exercise a restraint previously untested. For a brief moment he'd been furious that she'd chosen to dress in such a provocative manner and then he'd been forced to recall that her attire had been his selection, chosen in a desire to remind himself that he'd married a woman prepared to sell herself. Instead he'd succeeded in making her achingly sexy. With those huge, innocent eyes and those endless legs she'd caught the attention of every man in the club. Not used to dealing with jealousy, Sebastien had gritted his teeth and wrestled with the totally baffling impulse to cover her from head to foot in a giant bin bag before transporting her home in an armoured vehicle with blacked-out windows.

It had taken every ounce of self-control for him not to grab the man who'd been dancing and smiling at Alesia and knock him unconscious.

Faced with the fact that he'd married a woman who was a walking temptation, Sebastien vowed that if he ever displayed her in public again then she'd be wearing a sack.

Perhaps it was just that he now viewed Alesia as his property, he mused, and he'd never been that great at sharing. And discovering that his bride was every bit as hot-blooded as himself made him even more inclined to lock her in his tower and throw away the key.

His body heating to boiling point at the mere memory of her uninhibited response to him, Sebastien inhaled deeply and forced himself to acknowledge that although he usually considered himself exceptionally broad-minded about many things, his new wife didn't fall into that category. When it came to Alesia his attitude was completely and unashamedly Greek.

Dressed in a shimmer of silk that she guessed must have cost a fortune, Alesia stepped out on to the terrace and blinked in surprise.

The table was laid, candles flickered in the darkness and the air smelt enticingly of heat and summer. And she knew Sebastien had done it all for her.

'Drink?' Sebastien strolled towards her and handed her a glass, which she took with a wary smile.

'I'm not sure if I should—'

'It's not alcoholic,' he drawled lightly. 'I may be many things, *agape mou*, but stupid isn't one of them, although I have to confess that you become a different person under the influence of alcohol.'

She flushed. 'I enjoyed dancing—'

'So I observed.' He surveyed her steadily. 'I want to know why last night was your first visit to a nightclub. I want to know why you haven't shopped.'

She searched for inspiration. 'Do you spend everything you earn?'

A ghost of a smile touched his firm mouth. 'Hardly.'

'Precisely.' She gave a shrug. 'I don't know where you get this idea that money is all about shopping.'

'Perhaps because to the female sex it usually is,' he drawled, 'but you're teaching me that women are even more complex than I first thought.' He waved a hand at the table. 'Let's sit down.'

He was being so polite and she just wasn't used to it. Up until now their relationship had consisted of nothing but insults followed by hot sex.

She settled into her seat and her eyes scanned the various dishes laid out on the table. 'Did you cook?'

'Not exactly.' He gave a rueful smile. 'I confess that most of the dishes are delivered ready-made.'

'They look good.' She leaned forward and took a closer look in the dish nearest to her. 'Jannis makes the same thing. It's my favourite—'

Sebastien stilled, his powerful frame suddenly rigid with tension, stunning dark eyes suddenly icy-cold. '*Who* is Jannis?'

Alesia stared at him in surprise, wondering why he suddenly sounded so angry. 'Jannis is your chef.'

The tension left him. 'Of course.'

'He's been teaching me to cook Greek dishes,' Alesia told him, wondering what was the matter with him. 'I enjoy it.'

She just loved cooking and it was wonderful not to have to think about the cost of the ingredients.

Dark eyes swept over her. 'How else have you been spending your time in my absence?'

She shrugged. 'I explored Athens.'

'And?' His gaze was quizzical. 'Did you enjoy the experience?'

She smiled. 'It's an amazing city. Fascinating.'

He took a deep breath. 'How is it that you have never visited Athens before? Your grandfather has a home very near to mine. Surely you have visited him there?'

Alesia froze. 'I—no,' she said finally. 'I only ever saw him at his home on Corfu.'

Just the once.

Her heart started to beat faster. Would he think that was suspicious? Would he question her further?

'What about you?' Taking the initiative, she started to question him. 'I know you have several different homes.'

He gave a smile. 'Several different houses, *agape mou*, but only one home. This one.' He was silent for a moment, staring out across the lit terrace towards the sea. 'Home should be somewhere that you can be yourself. Somewhere private, a place where you don't have to answer to other people.'

'But you're rich,' she blurted out impulsively. 'You don't have to answer to anyone—'

He topped up her glass, a gleam of amusement in his eyes as he looked at her. 'I run an extremely complex, billion-dollar corporation,' he drawled, 'and on most days it feels as though I answer to the world. Decisions that I make have an effect on other people's employment—on their lives.'

And did that really matter to him? Did he really care? Alesia stared at him. 'My grandfather just made lots of people redundant—'

His mouth tightened and the amusement in his eyes faded, to be replaced by a steely expression. 'And those people had families and responsibilities of their own. Redundancy is a reflection of poor business planning. If you look into the future you can anticipate market changes and respond in time. Redeploy people if necessary, offer training. My company has never been forced to make redundancies.'

'And yet you have a reputation every bit as ruthless as my grandfather,' she replied unthinkingly and to her surprise he laughed.

'Well, I'm certainly no soft touch, *agape mou*,' he drawled lightly. 'I reward people well and in return I expect them to work hard. It's a fairly simple formula.'

And yet the financial pages of all the newspapers described him as a business genius. Alesia recalled the things she'd read about him following that first meeting with her grandfather.

'I read that when you left university you didn't join your father's business,' she said and he gave a shrug.

'It is never comfortable stepping into someone else's shoes. I was hotheaded. I wanted to prove myself on my own ground.'

'So you started your own business?'

'My father's business is very traditional,' he explained, leaning forward and filling her plate. 'I wanted to test other areas so I developed computer software with a friend from university and then we sold it to companies. In our first year we turned over fifty million dollars. We developed the company for several years and then sold it and by then I was ready to join my father. And that's enough about me. I want to hear about you. I have heard about English boarding schools.'

Alesia smiled and helped herself to more food. 'Actually, I loved it.' It was the only home she'd ever known.

He frowned sharply. 'It is true that you went there from the age of seven?'

'That's right.'

'That seems a very young age for a child.'

But she hadn't had a home. Her father had been killed.

Her mother was seriously ill in hospital and her grandfather had disowned her.

'I liked it.'

'You were never tempted to live with your grandfather?'

She almost laughed. *Live with her grandfather?* Did he really know so little about the man?

'I enjoyed my time at school.'

'And then you went straight to university?'

She nodded. 'I read music and French.'

He refilled her plate for the third time. 'You have an amazingly healthy appetite,' he observed with a faint smile and it was on the tip of her tongue to confess that she'd never seen so much food in her life before but she stopped herself in time.

Instead she smiled. 'I love Greek food.'

He looked at her with a curious expression in his eyes. 'I'm pleased.' He lounged back in his chair and questioned her more about her music and her courses and when she finally put her fork down he stood up and extended a hand.

'I want you to play my piano, *pethi mou.*' He hauled her to her feet and flashed her a smile. 'A private concert with only me in the audience.'

Her gaze collided with his and for a breathless moment she couldn't think about music or the piano. She couldn't think about anything except the sudden explosion of sexual need which engulfed her.

Sebastien gave a sensuous smile of all-male understanding. 'Later,' he breathed softly, leading her back into the main living area towards the piano. 'Now I want you to play for me.'

It was an order and she sat down at the piano stool and automatically flicked her hair so that it flowed down her back and not over the keys.

For a moment she sat in silence, staring at the familiar keys, her mind slightly detached.

And then she started to play. First Chopin, then Mozart, then Beethoven and finally Rachmaninov. Her fingers flew over the keys, fluent and nimble, stroking each note lovingly, drawing the best from the piano until eventually the final piece ended and her hands fell into her lap.

Silence followed.

Suddenly horribly aware that she hadn't even questioned him on his tastes, hadn't even thought to ask what he wanted to listen to, she risked a glance in his direction.

He was sprawled on the sofa, eyes closed, dense lashes brushing his sculpted cheekbones, long, powerful legs stretched out in front of him.

Alesia bit her lip in consternation. Had he fallen asleep?

'That was amazing.' His eyes opened reluctantly and she connected with blazing black. 'Truly amazing. I had no idea you could play like that. Why aren't you charging millions for public recitals?'

She swallowed and dragged her eyes away from his. 'I'm not famous—'

'But you *could* be,' he asserted, coming upright in a fluid movement and walking towards her. 'You could be world-famous.'

'I don't think so.' She looked away, embarrassed and *pleased* that he'd enjoyed her playing so much.

'You've just finished your degree—what now?' Sebastien enquired with the single-minded focus of someone who has his entire life clearly mapped out in front of him. 'Before you agreed to this marriage—what were your plans?'

To carry on holding down three jobs so that her mother could have the care she needed—

'I hadn't really thought—'

'Your grandfather didn't mention your talent,' Sebastien mused and Alesia clamped her jaws together and refrained from pointing out that her grandfather knew less than nothing about her. To him she was just a pawn. *You are the tool of my revenge.*

'I don't think my grandfather is very interested in music.'

'I adore your playing,' Sebastien said huskily, pulling her to her feet and framing her face with his hands. 'You are intensely passionate and sensitive—all the things that make you so wildly exciting in bed—'

Colour flew into her cheeks. 'Sebastien—'

'And I love the fact that you blush so easily,' he murmured, bending his dark head and capturing her mouth in a drugging kiss that sent a flash of the most intense sexual desire shooting through her.

She gave a soft moan and moved invitingly against his hard, powerful frame and as he whispered to her in Greek he swept her into his arms.

He was always doing this, she thought vaguely, her head still spinning from the after-effects of his erotic kiss, her limbs trembling as he strode through to the bedroom and lowered her into the middle of the bed.

'I can't get enough of you,' he groaned, sliding the tiny straps of her dress down her arms and fastening a burning kiss on her shoulder, 'and we're not leaving this island until I can go through at least five minutes in a business meeting without thinking of you.'

Fleetingly she remembered that she'd resolved not to let him do this to her again, and then his skilled fingers stripped her naked and his mouth found the sensitive jut of her nipple and the thought vanished, obliterated in an explosion of sexual excitement so intense that she sobbed his name.

'No woman has *ever* excited me the way you do,' he asserted in a raw tone, as his clever fingers proceeded to plot an erotic path down her quivering, hopelessly sensitized body. 'It is so hard to hold back.'

'Then *don't*,' she breathed unsteadily, her blue eyes glazed as she collided with his burning dark gaze.

'I don't want to hurt you—'

She closed her eyes, suffocated by the building desire, needing him so badly that her whole body ached and shivered. 'Sebastien, please—'

He gave a rough exclamation and rolled her under him in a swift, powerful movement, positioning himself between her thighs before he covered her mouth with his once more and took her.

The hot, hard strength of him deep inside her made her cry out in shameful abandon and he smothered the cry with his mouth, his own harsh grunt of male satisfaction mingling with her soft gasps.

He drove them both forward with powerful thrusts, smashing down any barriers that remained between them, an animal mating that culminated in explosive fulfilment for both of them.

In the aftermath Alesia lay with her eyes closed, waiting for him to release her, braced for his usual dismissive comment.

Instead he rolled on to his back, taking her with him, smoothing her tangled blonde hair away from her flushed cheeks with a hand that was far from steady.

'That was amazing,' he said hoarsely, studying her face. 'You are amazing. We can make this marriage work, Alesia.'

She swallowed. 'Because the sex is good—?'

'Not just because of that, but of course that is one reason,' he said, delivering a smile so sexy that she felt her whole body quiver. 'But I am fast discovering more and more about you. And I like what I discover.'

Suddenly consumed by guilt at the enormity of her deception, Alesia tried to wriggle away from him but he held her firm.

'No, this time I am not going to walk away. Nor will I say

anything horrible. We are going to spend the night together. In the same bed. I believe that children deserve parents who are happy together.' He dropped a lingering kiss on her mouth. 'I believe that we can be happy together.'

Guilt shot through her with the force of a bullet.

They couldn't be happy together. She couldn't give him children, and when he found that out... How could she tell him?

'You think I'm a gold-digger—'

He gave a dismissive shrug. 'At least you were honest about it. I can respect honesty. And what we share in bed is nothing to do with money, *agape mou*—'

He respected honesty.

Alesia closed her eyes, sick with dread at the thought of him discovering the truth.

That she'd been anything but honest with him.

But did he really need to find out? a tiny voice murmured inside her. She wouldn't be the first woman in the world who couldn't have children. Maybe he wouldn't discover that she'd always known...

CHAPTER EIGHT

THE week that followed was the most blissful time of Alesia's life.

They made love for most of the night and much of the day and when they weren't sleeping off the exhaustion induced by endless mind-blowing sex, they were talking or eating meals out on the terrace that overlooked the gentle curve of sand. And, to her surprise, Alesia discovered that she *loved* Greece. Even the constant view of the sea stretching into the distance couldn't spoil her delight at waking every morning to blazing sunshine. She adored exploring the island, adored picking oranges fresh from the tree and loved the feel of the sun on her skin.

And she also discovered that she *loved* talking to Sebastien.

He was astonishingly entertaining company and for the first time in her life she experienced what it was like to be close to another human being and it felt amazing.

On one occasion they didn't leave the bed but made love, slept and then just talked and talked while they lay wrapped around each other.

Sebastien proved to have a sharp wit, a brilliant mind and a good sense of humour as well as being astonishingly astute about the world. He was also charming and so incredibly sexy that Alesia found herself just gazing and gazing at his handsome face, unable to believe that this man was actually in bed with *her*.

Alone on the island, they were cocooned in their own sensual nest, protected from the interfering gaze of the outside world.

Protected from the looming clouds of reality.

Swamped with a quite unfamiliar feeling of happiness, Alesia drifted through each day on a cloud of pure bliss, dimly aware that this wasn't real—that this idyllic life they were sharing couldn't continue.

She was dozing in bed late one morning exactly one week after they'd first arrived on the island when Sebastien strolled into the room, vibrant and masculine and just pulsing with his usual energy.

Alesia forced herself awake, wishing that she had even a fraction of his apparently limitless energy. 'Sorry—' she yawned, brushing her hair away from her face and rubbing her eyes '—couldn't wake up this morning.'

'That's because of last night,' he teased, the sensual flash of his dark eyes a heated reminder of the intimacies they'd shared.

As she held his gaze, Alesia felt her stomach roll over and wondered if she'd ever be able to look at him without experiencing that intense burst of sexual excitement deep inside her. He only had to walk into a room and her insides fell away. Especially now when he was wearing only a pair of swimming shorts. He maintained a punishing exercise regime and the results showed in every pulsing inch of his impressive physique. From the broad, muscular shoulders to his lean, flat stomach and long legs, he had the most amazing body she'd ever seen and she couldn't look at him without wanting him to take her back to bed. It didn't matter that he didn't love her. It didn't matter that he thought she was a gold-digger. She was just *desperate* for him.

She was a *hopeless* case.

'I'll get up in a minute,' she promised, wishing that he'd suggest they spend yet another day in bed. It was the only place she wanted to be with him.

He surveyed her with amused eyes. 'I'm feeling shamefully guilty that we've been here for an entire week and you haven't swum in the pool once,' he teased, scooping her up and carrying her on to the terrace. 'I've kept you pinned to the bed and that isn't exactly fair.'

Staring dreamily at his staggeringly handsome face, it took a moment for Alesia to realize what he had in mind.

And by then it was too late to stop him.

She experienced a second of heart-stopping panic and then he dropped her into the pool and darkness closed around her.

Guilt-ridden and seriously worried for the first time in his life, Sebastien paced backwards and forwards across the marble floor while the doctor he'd had flown in examined a white-faced Alesia.

It had been little consolation to him when she'd recovered consciousness because she'd proceeded to shiver so violently that no amount of blankets seemed to warm her. It was as if the chill came from the inside.

'She's suffering from shock,' the doctor said calmly, finishing his examination and closing his bag. 'Physically she's fine. Swallowed a bit of water when she went under so she might be feeling a bit sick, but apart from that no lasting effects. Mentally it's another matter. At a guess I'd say that she suffers from a phobia about water. Probably wasn't such a good idea to drop her in the pool.'

Unaccustomed to being lectured or to being in the wrong, Sebastien gritted his teeth and took the criticism levelled at him with remarkable restraint.

Never in his life had he felt so utterly remorseful and if a sound telling off was what it took to make him feel better, then he was more than willing to take it on the chin.

He didn't care.

All he cared about was the fact that Alesia still looked as pale as the marble on his floors and that her eyes were haunted. And he *truly* wished the shivering would stop.

Reluctant to leave her alone for more than a few minutes,

he walked the doctor back to the waiting helicopter, a frown in his eyes. 'You're sure I shouldn't fly her back to Athens tonight?'

'My advice?' The doctor handed his bag to the pilot and looked Sebastien straight in the eye. 'She needs rest. I think you should keep her here tonight, give her time to get over the shock, then fly back tomorrow when she's feeling better.'

Pausing on the threshold of his living room, Sebastien noted grimly that her skin exactly matched his white sofas and decided to take the matter of her recovery into his own hands.

He strode over to a tray of drinks and closed lean bronzed fingers around a curving bottle.

Moments later he slipped an arm under Alesia's shoulders and scooped her up, making a mental note to instruct his chef to stuff her full of food on their return to Athens. She was far too fragile.

He lifted the glass to her dry lips. 'Drink.'

Obediently she took a sip and then choked and pulled a face.

'It's disgusting.'

'On the contrary, it's an extremely expensive brandy,' Sebastien informed her, his voice thick with strain as he lifted the glass to her lips again. 'You are still suffering from shock. Please drink.'

She took a few sips and then flopped back against the pillow, totally drained.

'I'm sorry—'

Laden with guilt that she was the one apologizing when it had been he who'd thrown her in the water, Sebastien raked shaking fingers through his still-damp dark hair.

'I'm the one who's sorry,' he said stiffly, unaccustomed to apologizing but determined to do so at the earliest possible minute in the hope that the incredible discomfort inside him would ease. 'But why didn't you tell me that you didn't swim—?'

She closed her eyes. 'I didn't go near the water—'

He gritted his teeth. All right, so he should have noticed that fact. 'It just didn't occur to me that it was because you were afraid—'

Her eyes stayed closed. 'Doesn't matter now.'

It mattered to him.

Driven by a need to put right a wrong, Sebastien disposed of the glass and scooped her on to his lap. 'I wish you would stop shivering,' he groaned but no matter how tightly he held her the shivering continued.

'Sorry—'

'Stop saying that,' he breathed in a raw tone, stroking her damp hair away from her face. 'I'm the one who is sorry but you should have told me how you felt. That first day when you were so afraid. I thought it was the flying, but I was barking up the wrong tree, wasn't I? It was the water—'

Her teeth chattering, she gave a reluctant nod and he cursed softly.

She closed her eyes. 'I'm being stupid—'

'You are not being stupid,' he said quietly. 'You are clearly reacting to something that happened in your past. I want to know what it was.'

There was a brief silence.

'I was on the boat—'

Sebastien tensed, unsure that he'd heard her correctly. 'What boat?'

'Your father's boat. The day it exploded. I was there. I almost drowned.'

Shattered by her unexpected confession, Sebastien found himself lost for words. 'That's not true,' he said finally, his voice sounding nothing like his own. 'There were no children invited on the boat that day—'

'I wasn't invited.' Still shivering, Alesia huddled deeper

in the blankets, her blue eyes blank of expression. 'I went on board only moments before the explosion. I was supposed to have stayed at the hotel in Athens with my nanny but I was desperate to show my mother a new doll I'd been given.'

Memories crowded into his brain. *A young child badly injured—*

'You were on board when the boat exploded?' His voice was hoarse and she lifted her head and nodded, her beautiful heart-shaped face so white that Sebastien momentarily toyed with instructing his pilot to return with the doctor immediately.

'I'd barely set foot on the boat,' she said softly, 'and my parents didn't know that I'd arrived.' She swallowed. 'I don't remember much, to be honest. I was only seven. I just remember standing on the gangplank one minute and then being plunged into water. It was everywhere—I thrashed and thrashed.' Her fingers clenched into her palms and she had to force herself to stay calm. 'I couldn't breathe, couldn't find air, felt terrible pain and then everything went black.'

Sebastien's breath hissed through his teeth and his face was pale under his tan. 'Someone rescued you—do you know who?'

'No.' She gave a wan smile. 'It was just a deckhand.'

'You were the only child on the boat that day—?'

She frowned. 'Yes—I suppose so.'

'*Theos mou*—' His voice was hoarse and he raked an unsteady hand through his glossy dark hair. 'I didn't know—'

'Didn't know what? What difference does it make?'

'You were injured? And you lost both of your parents.'

Her gaze slid guiltily away from his. 'I'm fine now.'

Sebastien surveyed her in frowning contemplation, sure that she wasn't telling him the truth. But why would she lie? Having confessed as much as she had, why would she now choose to conceal the truth about the accident?

'Sebastien?'

Aware that her teeth were still chattering, Sebastien's frown deepened. 'What?'

'Could we just go to bed?'

Faced with a potential solution which was well within his sphere of experience, Sebastien seized on the suggestion with enthusiasm and immediately lifted her into his arms.

'I could probably walk,' she murmured into his neck and he tightened his grip.

'Probably is not good enough,' he growled, lowering her on to the bed as if she were made of something extremely fragile and covering her with a sheet.

Her eyes flew to his. 'Aren't you joining me?'

Humbled by the question, Sebastien inhaled deeply. 'Do you want me to? I dropped you in the water—'

She gave a tired smile. 'You didn't know—'

'But I know now and from now on nothing is going to hurt you, *agape mou*,' Sebastien vowed, stripping off and joining her in the bed with a flattering degree of speed.

With characteristic decisiveness he hauled her against him and rearranged her so that every shivering inch of her was pressed against his own body.

'Feels nice,' she mumbled, her eyes closing as she nestled against his shoulder.

Discovering feelings of protectiveness which he hadn't known he was capable of, Sebastien lay still, afraid to move in case the shivering started again.

No wonder she'd hated his family, he mused grimly, breathing in her warm, tantalizing scent and forcing himself to ignore it.

And no wonder Dimitrios Philipos blamed the Fiorukis family for everything. Not only had his beloved only son been killed on the Fiorukis yacht along with his wife, but the last remaining member of his family, his precious grand-daughter, had been injured.

Was that why he'd had her educated in England? Sebastien mused.

Had Philipos removed her from Greece for her own safety?

Clearly he'd misjudged Dimitrios Philipos, Sebastien conceded, stroking aside a strand of blonde hair from Alesia's face and noting with relief that her colour was showing a definite improvement. In choosing to link their two families then he was indeed healing a rift that had been painful for both parties.

And, once he'd consulted experts and cured her of her water phobia, their marriage could begin properly.

Starting from tomorrow, Sebastien vowed, they were going to be a proper family.

Alesia held tightly to Sebastien's hand, grateful for the distraction that his conversation offered. He'd already apologized about a hundred times for the fact that they had to board the helicopter in order to return to Athens but he'd assured her that the alternative boat trip was much longer and would be more agonizing for her.

Touched by his concern and feeling much safer than she could have imagined possible, Alesia kept hold of his hand and forced herself to concentrate on other things as the azure-blue Mediterranean blurred beneath them.

Traumatic though the incident had been, she was glad that he knew. In a way she'd revealed an important part of herself. And if anything they were closer than ever and she knew now that she loved Sebastien Fiorukis with a wild passion that she hadn't believed possible.

Never had she thought she'd share this with a man and if, deep down, part of her was constantly reminding her that she wasn't being totally honest with him, she was managing to ignore it.

For the first time in her life she was *truly* happy and she wasn't going to allow anything to spoil it.

Sebastien's mobile phone rang as soon as they landed and he gave a frustrated sigh. 'End of our peace and quiet,' he drawled as he shot her a look of apology and took the call.

Alesia smiled. She didn't mind that he took the call. She understood his dedication to his business, the fact that he cared what happened to his employees, the fact that he took his responsibilities so seriously. It was one of the many qualities that she'd grown to love about him.

Sebastien ended the call and looked at her, indecision evident in every plane of his handsome face.

'What's the matter?' Relieved to finally be on dry land, Alesia relaxed.

'That was the office.' He gave a rueful smile. 'A crisis awaits—'

'Then you should go.'

'I don't want to leave you,' he confessed, his dark eyes sweeping her face with visible concern. 'You were so unwell yesterday and I feel totally responsible.'

Basking in the totally new experience of having someone who wanted to take care of her, Alesia smiled at him happily. 'I'm fine now. I'll just rest and wait for you to come home,' she assured him, thinking that his absence would give her time to phone her mother and experiment with all those wonderful new cosmetics he'd presented her with. Hopefully the rack of clothes would still be there too, and she'd be able to wow him with an amazing outfit on his return from the office.

'I won't be long,' he promised, bending his dark head to deliver a drugging kiss to her parted lips, 'and if you feel at all ill you're to call me on my mobile.'

'I don't know the number.'

He looked startled, as if it hadn't occurred to him before now that she'd had no way of getting in touch with him. 'I'll get you a phone straight away, with my number programmed into it. The slightest problem, I want you to call.'

With visible reluctance he strode back towards the waiting helicopter without bothering to change.

That must be one of the benefits of being the boss, Alesia mused, watching in a fog of total infatuation as he boarded the helicopter again. You could dress any way you liked. Not that Sebastien needed clothes to give him stature. He oozed confidence from every taut muscle of his amazing body. He could have been dressed in a bin bag and it still would have been obvious who was in charge.

Recalling just how long it had taken her to apply her make-up on the previous occasion, Alesia hurried up to their bedroom and walked into the dressing room, noticing with considerable disappointment that the rack of clothes had disappeared. The only outfit remaining was the skimpy skirt and top she'd worn for the nightclub.

She studied it thoughtfully. She'd loved that outfit and she was pretty sure that Sebastien had loved it too. Why not wear it again? First they'd have dinner, then perhaps he'd take her to another nightclub and they could dance and dance and after that—

Delighted with her own idea, Alesia virtually skipped down the stairs to discuss suitable dinner menus with Jannis, Sebastien's head chef, and then returned to their bedroom suite to begin the transformation she had planned.

She bathed in richly scented water, daydreamed about Sebastien and smiled at the thought of the evening ahead. This time she managed her make-up in half the time and was reasonably pleased with the result. Feeling transformed and extremely feminine, she slipped her feet into the same pair of shoes that she'd worn dancing, vowing that this evening she'd remove them and dance in bare feet.

Once she was ready she settled down to wait for Sebastien. And she waited.

Twice she picked up the phone he'd had delivered to her and stood with her finger poised over the right button only to return the phone to the table with a sigh of frustration. She wasn't going to phone him to ask him when he was coming home. He'd said that he'd be as quick as he could. She didn't want him to think she was clingy.

More time passed and Alesia chewed her lip and paced backwards and forwards in their bedroom. He was an important man, she reasoned, and he'd been away for an entire week. It was only natural that he needed some time in the office. Loads of people probably needed to talk to him.

By the time the sun went down her fingers were once again itching to pick up the phone. Why didn't he at least *call*? Had she misunderstood his desire to be home early?

Then she heard footsteps outside and the bedroom door crashed open. Sebastien stood there, dark stubble grazing his hard jaw, his dark eyes glittering dangerously in the dim light.

He looked remote, distant and thoroughly intimidating and nothing like the man she'd spent the last week with.

Alesia looked at him warily. 'Y-you don't look as though you had a great day,' she said nervously and in response he strode into the room and slammed the door shut behind him.

Alesia winced. 'If you're hungry, then—'

'I'm not hungry.' His voice was lethally smooth and he paced towards her, his shimmering dark gaze never leaving her face. 'Aren't you going to ask me if I had an interesting day at the office, *agape mou*?'

She shivered slightly at his tone and instinctively took a step backwards. 'You're very late so I expect you were busy—'

'Extremely busy.' His tone was almost conversational. 'Busy discovering plenty of interesting facts about my new wife. Facts which she hadn't thought to reveal herself even though we've just spent a week getting to know each other.'

Alesia felt the colour drain out of her face.

How much did he know?

'Sebastien—'

She couldn't believe how different he was from the man who'd been so concerned about leaving her only half a day earlier. Gone was the warmth and consideration that she'd enjoyed so much. In its place was cold disdain.

But was that really so surprising?

How could she have thought that this fairy-tale existence could continue when it was built on such shaky foundations? A good relationship needed trust and honesty and she'd given him lies and falsehoods. Nothing built on that could be sustained. It was inevitable that it would come crashing down in spectacular style.

'Perhaps you'd better tell me what you're talking about,' she said stiffly and he gave a cynical laugh.

'Why? So you can work out what I already know so that you don't reveal more than you have to? Don't worry, *agape mou*, I already know just how good you are at keeping secrets. I learned today a number of interesting facts about your life. Like the fact that up until two weeks before our wedding you have had no contact with your grandfather since you were *seven years old*.' His expression grim, he fixed her with his chilly dark gaze. 'So who paid the fees for that expensive school you attended?'

Feeling sicker by the minute, Alesia forced her voice to work. 'I won a music scholarship,' she croaked. 'There were no fees.'

He registered that admission by a tensing of his broad shoulders. 'And, according to my sources, once you were at university you held down no fewer than *three* jobs. You had two waitress jobs and you played the piano in a bar. *How* did you achieve your degree? When did you do any studying?'

'I was often exhausted,' she confessed with a glimmer of a smile that faded as soon as she registered his blackening expression. He was *furiously* angry with her. 'I'm not afraid of hard work.'

'Well, that, at least, is one thing in your favour,' he bit out harshly and she shrank slightly. Clearly he didn't think there was much else.

'Most students take one job,' he growled, pacing across the floor like a man at the very limits of his patience, 'and I can understand that you needed money because you had no parents to provide for you and a grandfather who refused to acknowledge your existence, but why *three*? What did you do with the money?' His eyes slid over her in silent question. 'All the clothes you possess, I bought you with the exception of your wedding dress. You don't shop and you're so fragile that you *clearly* don't eat much.'

Her gaze shifted from his and she swallowed. 'General living costs—'

'*General living costs?*' He stopped dead and repeated her words slowly, as if he were struggling with his English, and the tone he used revealed just how ridiculous he found her mumbled statement. 'Presumably this is why you went along with this deception and agreed to the marriage. Why should you struggle financially when a simpler, more lucrative option was available to you?'

She winced. Once again he made her sound just *awful*, as though the only thing she ever thought of was money. She wanted to tell him about her mother but she just couldn't; it wasn't her secret to divulge.

Sebastien started pacing again, the growing tension in his powerful frame clearly making it impossible for him to stand still. 'But the question I really want answered is why your grandfather wanted this marriage,' he growled. 'As I suspected at the beginning, he was *not* playing Happy Families by pursuing the idea of a match between us. Clearly he has no concern for your welfare whatsoever. You are merely a pawn in his evil game, although clearly a very willing pawn.

And now I want to know what the game is, Alesia. For once I want the truth.'

Alesia stared at him, appalled. Her life was collapsing in front of her eyes. To tell him would ruin everything that they'd built over the last few weeks and she just didn't want that to happen. She knew now that Sebastien was *nothing* like her grandfather. He was a responsible man with a strong sense of family and duty and fairness. And above all else he respected honesty. How could she confess that she'd deceived him in the cruellest way possible?

So how did she confess the enormity of her crime to a man like that?

The irony made her eyes sting with tears.

She loved him.

She loved him and she had to tell him probably the worst thing that a wife could tell a Greek man. He would never understand the desperation that had driven her to such a distasteful action. Their short, bittersweet relationship would be over virtually before it had started.

She started to shake so badly that she could no longer stand up. 'Sebastien—'

'Just one look at your ashen face warns me that I'm not going to like what you're about to tell me,' he bit out grimly, striding over to a small table and pouring himself a large whisky. 'I knew there was something more behind this "deal" but my father is an old man and was determined to end the feud once and for all. Stupidly, I went against my better judgement and decided to trust him.'

Alesia closed her eyes and wished she was somewhere else. Anywhere else.

Sebastien downed the drink in one and strode back over to her, the expression on his handsome face utterly forbidding. 'Since he clearly wasn't bothered whether you lived or died,' he said harshly, 'presumably your caring, devoted grandfather never wanted great-grandchildren either. And, since that was his stated reason for desiring this marriage, then I assume that his method of revenge must be somehow linked. Am I right?'

Alesia felt the nausea rise in her stomach. She was going to have to tell him. She was going to—

'Alesia—?' His tone was a sharp command and her eyes flew open and she lifted her chin.

This was her crime. Indefensible, but still her crime. She had to stand by what she'd done.

'The explosion left me badly injured,' she told him, just hating the fact that her voice was shaking so badly. 'The doctors said I would never be able to have children.'

Registering that announcement, Sebastien stood in rigid stillness, every muscle in his powerful body tense as he watched her. 'Just what exactly are you saying?' he asked hoarsely and she felt a lump building in her throat as she forced the words out.

'I can't give you children, Sebastien. Ever. It isn't possible.'

He inhaled deeply. 'And your grandfather somehow knew this?'

She nodded bleakly. 'My grandfather knows everything—'

Sebastien gave a harsh laugh and ran a hand over the back of his neck in a visible effort to relieve the tension. 'This, then, was his latest revenge. To deprive my parents of the grandchildren they long for so badly and to deprive me of a child.' He paced the length of the room one more time and made a sound of disbelief before he turned and fastened her with incredulous eyes. 'And you agreed to this? Your grandfather is renowned as an evil, manipulative man with no morals. But you? For the right sum of money, you were prepared to go ahead with this deception?'

Alesia shrank inside herself and stared at the floor in utter misery.

What could she say? The answer was quite obviously yes and she wasn't in a position to explain why the money had been so very important to her.

He made a sound of derision. 'Whatever my family may have done to yours, there is no excuse for that level of dishonesty.' His voice was thick with barely contained anger, streaks of colour accentuating his fabulous bone structure. It was as if something was about to explode inside him. 'How could I ever have thought a relationship was possible? Not only are you a gold-digger but you are also a liar and a cheat.'

'You can divorce me,' she whispered in anguish and he turned on her, raw anger blazing from his dark eyes.

'I *cannot* divorce you,' he contradicted her savagely, one lean brown hand slicing through the air to emphasize his point. 'Your scheming grandfather ensured that. The contract we both signed binds us together until you produce a child.'

Alesia swallowed painfully. 'I know I did wrong, but you have to understand—'

'Understand what?' He cut through her whispered attempt to defend herself with ill-concealed derision. 'That I married a woman completely bereft of human decency? I should have been more wary of your lineage. The Philipos blood runs in your veins and you have clearly inherited his complete lack of moral code.'

Driven by disgust that he didn't even attempt to hide, he strode out of the room, slamming the door shut behind him, leaving Alesia numb with horror.

CHAPTER NINE

ALESIA spent a sleepless night feeling sicker and sicker and *totally* miserable. Remembering what the doctor had said about her swallowing water when she'd fallen in the swimming pool, she assumed the nausea would go away at some point and tried to ignore it.

She longed to find Sebastien but she had no idea where to look for him and she wouldn't have known what to say even if she found him.

She was guilty as charged.

She had deceived him. She had lied. She had married him for money.

He was right. How could she possibly defend the indefensible?

His opinion of her shouldn't have mattered, but somewhere along the way she'd fallen crazily in love with him and the knowledge that he clearly hated her depressed her in the extreme.

The situation was irretrievably bad and she'd already decided that she might as well leave and go back to London when he stalked into her bedroom, dressed in a sleek designer suit, looking every inch the successful billionaire businessman that he was.

Struggling with nausea that refused to shift, Alesia sat up in bed, trying not to let the longing show in her face. The fact that she wanted him so badly that she ached wasn't relevant. He didn't want her.

'I'll leave today,' she said shakily, unable to hold that penetrating dark gaze for more than a few painful seconds. 'You can't divorce me but you don't have to live with me and I promise I'll—'

'I came to apologize,' he muttered stiffly, cutting through her awkward attempt to bridge the silence between them with his customary impatience. 'Last night I lost my temper. There's no excuse for that.'

He was apologizing to *her*?

She blinked. 'You have every right to be angry—'

'Last night you looked very ill—' His gaze swept over her and a frown touched his bronzed forehead. 'You still look ill.'

She gave a wan smile. 'I think it was just swallowing the water—I feel a bit sick, but I'm fine—'

His eyes slid back to hers but the frown remained. 'Today you must rest. Spend the day in bed,' he ordered, his tone cool and formal. 'We'll talk later.'

She gave a sigh. She felt flattened and exhausted by the intense outpouring of emotion. 'There's nothing to talk about, Sebastien,' she said quietly. 'We both know that. You clearly can't bear being in the same room as me, so I'll leave today.'

For some reason his tension seemed to increase. 'I don't want you to leave,' he breathed, tension spreading through his powerful frame and making the air throb and sizzle. 'You are my wife.'

'A wife who can't give you children,' she reminded him painfully, and he inhaled deeply.

'That may be true, but you are still my wife and you will *not* leave.'

Alesia felt her insides give a leap. Was he thinking about how happy their week together had been? Was he growing fond of her? Was he—

'Last night I was so angered by what I had heard I wasn't thinking clearly,' he confessed in a raw tone, turning away from her and pacing towards the window. 'But on reflection I can see that you have led an extraordinarily difficult life.

Because of the accident on my parents' boat you were left orphaned at a shockingly young age with no means of financial support. All your life you have worked and slaved to keep a roof over your head and food on the table. It is hardly surprising that, presented with an opportunity to improve your circumstances, you took it. You blamed my family for the death of your parents and for your own injuries.'

'Sebastien—'

'Let me finish,' Sebastien interrupted. He turned and dark eyes collided with hers. 'Whatever caused the explosion, my family was ultimately responsible for what happened that day and we should take responsibility for that.'

She swallowed painfully. 'What are you saying?'

'That you have a right to the life you have chosen,' he said stiffly, turning again and staring out of the window. 'My family owes you and I intend to honour that debt. You will remain as my wife and you will continue to receive the allowance we agreed. How you spend it is entirely your decision.'

Flayed by the knowledge that his desire for her to remain as his wife was driven totally by his sense of responsibility rather than anything deeper or more personal, Alesia flopped back against the pillows.

She didn't want to stay here under those circumstances and yet how could she do anything else? She needed Sebastien's money to support her mother. She had no choice but to stay. And if he hated her for what she'd done—well, she'd just have to live with that.

The next few weeks dragged by.

Sebastien spent most of his time at the office and returned home after she'd fallen asleep. He slept in a different room, as if to emphasize the fact that he could no longer stand the sight of her.

Days passed without them laying eyes on each other and,

on the rare occasions that they met at a meal table, he was polite and courteous but kept a distance that filled Alesia with utter misery. His tense civility was worse than his anger.

And, to make matters worse, the sickness hadn't passed as the doctor had predicted. If anything it was worse but she hid the fact from Sebastien because she knew that he already felt ridden with guilt for having thrown her in the swimming pool.

The final straw came when she rang the hospital to check on her mother only to be told that she'd developed a rare infection and was dangerously ill.

Stricken with guilt that she hadn't somehow contrived to visit her mother before now, Alesia packed a bag and asked Sebastien's driver to take her to the airport.

The chances were he wouldn't miss her, she reasoned as she watched Athens slide past from the comfort of the passenger seat. She knew he had a business meeting in Paris because she'd watched him board the helicopter that morning from the window in the drawing room.

Like a lovesick teenager, she often stared out of the windows of his Athenian villa, hoping for a glimpse of him.

How had this happened?

How had she managed to fall in love with him?

But she knew the answer to that, of course. From the moment she'd first laid eyes on him the extraordinary tension had been there between them. She'd entered the marriage full of contempt and determined to hate him, but those feelings had rapidly grown into something very different.

When she'd sorted out this latest crisis with her mother, she'd find a way of getting over Sebastien, she vowed as she slid out of the car with her small bag and quickly dismissed the bodyguard who had insisted on accompanying her to the airport.

She spent the whole flight to London trying not to be sick and decided that as soon as she got the chance she was going to have to consult a doctor. She must have picked up some bug or other from the water she'd swallowed.

When she arrived in London it was pouring with rain, the sky cloudy and ominously grey. Thinking bleakly that the weather suited her mood, she took a taxi into London and arrived at the top hospital in time to talk to the doctor who was in charge of her mother's care.

'How is she?' she asked anxiously and he gave her a sympathetic smile.

'It was a big operation, as you know, but she came through it well until the last few days. Unfortunately she's picked up a bug and we're running a series of tests to identify the cause.'

'Can I see her?'

'If you're Alesia then you are more than welcome,' the doctor said immediately. 'She talks about you constantly. I understand you've been working abroad?'

Alesia flushed. That was the story she'd given her mother as an excuse for not visiting before but suddenly she felt torn by guilt. She should have tried to come sooner—

But how could she? In order to fulfil the contract and get the money she'd had to play a role and without that money her mother couldn't have had the operation.

Deciding that life was one long round of impossible decisions, Alesia followed the nurse to her mother's room, tugging off her wedding ring as an afterthought and dropping it into her pocket.

At this moment in time her mother didn't need to know that she'd married a Fiorukis.

Her first sight of the fragile, pale woman in the hospital bed made her choke back tears and she struggled for control. Her mother had enough to worry about without having to comfort her.

'Mum?'

Her mother's eyes flew open at the sound of Alesia's voice

and a wonderful smile spread across her pale face. 'Darling! I didn't expect you to visit.' Her voice was so weak it was barely audible. 'You thought you might not be able to for a while.'

'It's fine.' Alesia swallowed hard and hurried across the room to give her mother a hug. 'You've lost so much weight.'

'Hospital food,' her mother joked weakly, lifting a hand to stroke her daughter's hair. 'You look tired. And pale. Have you been working too hard? How's the new job working out?'

'It's great,' Alesia said, avoiding eye-contact and settling herself in a chair that had been placed beside the bed.

Her mother gave a sigh and her eyes drifted shut again. 'Well, it was lucky for both of us that you got yourself that job when you did. And that it pays so well. If it weren't for you—'

'Don't. I love you.' Alesia gave a wobbly smile. 'And I *hated* not being able to visit you—'

'But you phoned every day,' her mother murmured, 'and you gave me the greatest gift that there is. The chance to walk again. Now we just have to wait and see whether the doctors have succeeded. Until this infection they were optimistic.'

'They're still optimistic.' Alesia felt her eyes fill and struggled to hold back the tears.

'Don't cry.' Her mother's voice was gruff. 'I rely on you to be strong. You've always been so strong. Even as a little girl you were fiercely determined.'

Alesia forced a smile. She didn't feel strong or determined. She felt sliced into pieces after the events of the last few weeks, but she knew she couldn't unburden herself on her mother. 'I'm fine. Just a bit tired.'

And ill. She felt *so* sick.

'How much time off have you been given?'

'As much as she needs.' A deep masculine drawl came from the doorway of the hospital room and Alesia sprang to her feet in shock, her heart suddenly thudding at an alarming rate as she stared at Sebastien.

He stood in the doorway, grim-faced and almost unbearably handsome, his lean, dark features set in anger. Gone was his characteristic cool. With one flash of those molten black eyes he told her everything she needed to know. That he was furious with her.

And then he dragged his gaze away from her, focused on her mother and the air hissed between his teeth. '*Theos mou*—I had no idea. You are *alive*. You survived the explosion.'

Alesia felt her insides plummet in panic. This was one scenario that she hadn't prepared herself for. 'I thought you were in Paris—'

'Tracking my moves, Alesia?' His eyes locked with hers, the derision in his gaze intensifying her guilt. 'Well, now I'm back—'

Before she could find a suitable answer, her mother gave a strangled moan and covered her mouth with her hand.

Immediately Alesia forgot about Sebastien. 'Mum?' She leaned forward and felt her mother's forehead, just frantic with worry. 'Are you feeling worse? Are you sick? I'll call a nurse.' She reached for the buzzer but her mother caught her hand.

'No.' Her voice sounded scratchy and her eyes were fixed on Sebastien. 'For years I've thought about you. In my dreams. In my darkest moments. You were always there.'

Alesia looked at her mother in consternation. She hadn't expected her to recognize Sebastien but clearly she did and it was equally clear that she *hated* him. The last thing she needed now was this sort of shock and it was all Alesia's fault.

She should have guessed that Sebastien would follow her.

She never should have come.

She turned to Sebastien, desperate to rescue such a disastrous situation. 'You're upsetting her. I think you should leave,' she pleaded urgently, taking her mother's hand in her own and squeezing it tightly. 'We can talk later—'

'If that is what your mother wants, then of course I will respect her wishes,' Sebastien said roughly, walking into the room with his customary air of purpose. 'But there are clearly things that need to be said.' He turned to Alesia's mother. 'I had no idea you were alive.'

Alesia closed her eyes. They just didn't talk about the accident any more. Her mother found it all too distressing. '*Please*, will you go—?'

'I don't want him to go.' Instead her mother stretched out a hand towards Sebastien, her blue eyes so like her daughter's brimming with unshed tears. 'Not until I've thanked him. If you only knew how much I've longed to thank him but I had no way of discovering who he was and tracing him. I didn't know his name—'

At that confusing declaration Alesia stared in astonishment and, to her surprise, Sebastien stepped up to the bed and took the hand that was offered, enveloping slender fingers with his own large, strong hand. 'No thanks are needed. Not then and not now—and I had no idea who *you* were until very recently.'

'There were so many people on the yacht that day—'

Alesia glanced between them in confusion. 'Mum—?'

'How did you make contact with him?' Her mother turned towards her and the tears spilled over and trickled down her pale cheeks. 'You knew how much I wanted to find the man who rescued me. Without a name, how did you ever find him, you clever girl?'

The man who had rescued her?

Stunned into silence, Alesia sat still, unable to speak or move for a long moment. When she finally managed to produce words, her voice was croaky. 'This was the man who rescued you when the boat exploded?'

That couldn't be true.

It couldn't have been Sebastien.

'And you. He rescued you too,' her mother said, a tremulous smile on her face as she looked at Sebastien. 'He risked his life so many times going under the water to find you. I saw you on the gangplank only seconds before the explosion. I knew you were in the water, probably too badly injured to help yourself. I was screaming and screaming for someone to save my baby.'

'Your mother was trapped under wreckage on the boat,' Sebastien said gruffly, his dark eyes shadowed by the memory. 'She refused to cooperate with any sort of rescue until I'd found her daughter.'

Alesia was in shock. The vision in her head. The man she remembered. 'It was you?' Her voice was barely audible. 'The man who rescued me—the man I remember—*that was you?*'

His jaw tightened. 'I didn't realize myself until the night when you told me your story,' Sebastien confessed, lines of tension visible around his dark eyes. 'I realized then that it had to have been your mother that I'd rescued but I had no idea that she was still alive. Philipos informed everyone that she had died along with Costas.'

'That's what he wanted people to believe. He wanted me out of his life. You went back on to the boat to rescue others,' Alesia's mother said quietly, 'and the ambulance took the two of us to hospital. I asked everyone about you but no one knew anything. Then Dimitrios had us flown to England and I was forbidden from ever visiting Greece again. We kept our identity secret under his instructions.'

Sebastien frowned, every inch of him suddenly alert. 'How could he make such a threat? How could he prevent you from visiting? And why?'

Her mother closed her eyes. 'He hated me from the first moment that Costas brought me home to Corfu. When Costas was killed there was no one to defend me. He threatened to take Alesia from me,' she said wearily, 'and bring her up as a Greek. As his own. He didn't really want her. It was just a threat to punish me. Few people know just how evil that man is. There was no way I wanted him near my daughter. I agreed to disappear. To break all contact. It suited him. It was what he always wanted.'

'He paid you to disappear?' Sebastien's eyes darkened with shock and disapproval and Charlotte Rawlings gave a tired laugh.

'Pay? Dimitrios? That shows how little you know him. No, he didn't pay me a penny.'

Sebastien stilled. 'But you were severely injured with a young daughter to support—how did you manage? You had family of your own to care for you?'

'I had no family, and I managed because my daughter is a unique and very special person,' Charlotte said in a gruff voice and Alesia coloured.

'Mum, I think you should rest now—'

'Not yet.' Sebastien tightened his hand around her mother's. 'Please—if you can manage it, I really need to hear the rest of this story.'

'Alesia recovered remarkably quickly from her injuries and she was a bright little thing.' Charlotte smiled lovingly at her daughter. 'One of the doctors who was treating me and knew our circumstances suggested she try for a scholarship at a top boarding school. She was accepted. It was a difficult decision but the right one. I was having endless operations. In the holidays she stayed with one of her tutors and they brought her to see me all the time.'

Sebastien was listening intently, all his attention focused on her face. 'Go on—'

'By the time she went to university I needed all sorts of

care that we had to pay for.' Charlotte shot her daughter a tortured look. 'Alesia worked night and day to provide for me. She would do *anything*. And when she discovered that there was a chance that this operation could help me walk again she got herself this amazing job in Greece—'

A tense silence followed that announcement and Alesia closed her eyes, waiting for Sebastien to tell her mother the truth.

'You should rest now,' he said calmly, standing up and arranging the sheets more comfortably around her mother, 'but before we leave you for a while, I have one more question. Why, when Alesia grew up and he could no longer take her away, did you not ask Philipos for money once again? You are his only family. He had a duty to provide for you.'

'Dimitrios knows nothing about duty and he never gives away money,' her mother said with quiet dignity. 'And he doesn't know the meaning of family.'

Something dark and dangerous flickered in Sebastien's eyes. 'Then it's time he was educated on that subject,' he said grimly, straightening to his full height, dominating the small hospital room with his powerful presence. 'And I can assure you that he will be a willing pupil. He *will* live up to his responsibilities.'

Charlotte Rawlings closed her eyes wearily. 'No. I want no contact with that man. I never want to hear the names Philipos or Fiorukis again.'

Alesia froze in horror. Although her mother obviously recognized Sebastien as the man who'd rescued her from the explosion, she clearly didn't know his identity. What would her mother say when she realized that her daughter had married a Fiorukis? And that she'd approached her grandfather for money?

Sebastien gave a calm, reassuring smile. 'I want you to rest and stop worrying,' he instructed firmly, 'and I will bring Alesia back tomorrow.'

Her mother opened her eyes and smiled. 'You can stay another day?' Her eyes brightened. 'When do you have to go back?'

Sebastien frowned. 'She can stay as long as she needs to,' he said roughly and then walked out of the room.

Alesia gave her mother a hug and then hurried after him, virtually running so that she could match his long stride.

'Sebastien, *wait*!' Breathless, she caught his arm, forcing him to stop. '*Please* don't just walk off. I know you're still angry with me but we have to talk. You saved my life. *I can't believe it was you.*'

Burning dark eyes collided with hers and he caught her arms and backed her against the nearest wall, his whole body throbbing with barely contained fury. 'And we would have discovered that fact a whole lot sooner if you'd been honest with me. *When* will you learn to trust me and tell me the truth?' he demanded in a raw undertone, his strong fingers biting into her soft flesh as he kept her pinned against the wall. 'On a daily basis I learn something new about my wife and the process is exhausting. Each time the phone rings I wonder what amazing fact I am about to discover that you have kept hidden. Until I met you I thought that I had an incredibly effective intelligence network. Suddenly I discover that I know *nothing*.'

'You probably weren't looking in the right place,' Alesia muttered awkwardly, realizing that for a man accustomed to being in control all these revelations must be difficult to cope with. 'You didn't know my mother was alive.'

'That's right, I didn't.' He stared at her with naked exasperation. '*Why* did you hide that fact from me? And the fact that *you* were on the boat too?'

She lifted a hand to her throbbing forehead, desperate to make him understand. 'Because if I'd told you the truth you would have known that we were anything but a happy family. And if you'd known that my grandfather *despised* me, then you would have known that his desire for a union between us was driven by a desire for revenge, not grandchildren to bounce on his knee. I was too scared to tell you the truth.' She swallowed hard, breathlessly aware of every inch of his hard body pressed against hers. *She'd missed him so much.* 'And then you wouldn't have married me. And I needed you to marry me. It was the only way I could see to get the money for my mother's operation. It's a really new procedure and the NHS wouldn't fund it. I was *desperate*.'

She'd been totally out of her depth.

'I should have picked up the signals at that first meeting,' Sebastien growled, his brows locked in an ominous frown as he listened to her. 'You were so clearly afraid of him but my father was longing to have the company returned to him and I was distracted by certain other matters. Otherwise I would have realized that something wasn't right.'

Wondering what other matters had distracted him, Alesia gave a tired smile. 'Well, you know it all now,' she said, her head swimming as his familiar male scent wrapped itself around her brain and teased her senses. When he stood this close she couldn't concentrate. 'I *did* marry you for the money but I wanted the money for my mother. There was no other way. My grandfather has refused to acknowledge her existence since the day she married my father.'

'Your grandfather has a great deal to answer for,' Sebastien said grimly, inhaling deeply as he struggled for control. Aware that several nurses were glancing in their direction, he released her. 'This is not the place to have the discussion we need to have. Let's get out of here.'

He closed long, strong fingers around her wrist and virtually dragged her towards the nearest lift. With disbelief he scanned the ancient lift and instead opted for the stairs. 'If that thing breaks down we'll be in it for ever,' he growled. 'And what *is* this hospital? It looks as though it is about to fall down.'

'It is a very old building,' Alesia agreed breathlessly, wishing she had legs as long as his, 'but the surgeon here has an amazing reputation and he wanted to try something that had never been tried before. That's how I spent your money.'

'*Your* money,' he corrected her, a strange expression in his eyes as he shouldered open the door and held it for her to pass through. 'It was your money. And finally I understand why you didn't go shopping. You didn't have any left to buy anything for yourself.'

She blushed. 'I didn't need anything. And the hospital is very expensive—'

He looked around with an ironic gleam in his eyes. 'I can't understand why,' he drawled, leading her across the foyer and straight into his car, which was parked directly outside. 'It looks as though it should have been demolished years ago.'

'How did you know where to find me?'

'You were followed,' he told her grimly, leaning across to fasten her seat belt. 'My security team were under strict instructions not to let you out of their sight.'

She gazed at him in astonishment. 'Why?'

'Because you are a Fiorukis now,' he reminded her in a dry tone, the exasperated gleam in his dark gaze revealing just how naïve he found her question, 'and there are plenty of people willing to cash in on that.'

Her eyes widened. 'You think someone might kidnap me?'

'The possibility is always there but you needn't worry too much,' he drawled with a faint smile. 'They would release you soon enough when they discover how much you eat.'

She bit her lip as she studied his tense expression. 'Are you very angry with me?'

'You have driven me to the extreme of emotion since the day we met, so this is nothing new,' he murmured huskily. 'And, for future reference, the next time you wish to fly, use my plane. Like it or not, you are my wife and I won't have my wife taking a commercial flight.'

A warm feeling spread through her. She should have felt angry that he was giving orders again but after a lifetime of making her own decisions it felt wonderful for someone else to take charge. Part of her loved the fact that he was so possessive. And she basked in his determination to take care of her, even though she knew that it was only driven by his sense of responsibility towards her.

Cocooned in the luxury of Sebastien's car, Alesia stared out of the window, watching the sights of London pass by. 'Oh, look! There's the Monument. It was built to commemorate the Great Fire of London.' She gazed upwards to the viewing area. 'I remember my mother taking me there on one of her rare periods out of the hospital. I climbed all the way up to the top, all three hundred and eleven steps, while she waited in the street and waved.'

Slightly choked by the memory, she met Sebastien's eye and gave a wobbly smile.

He hesitated and then reached out and took her hand in his. 'You must have missed her dreadfully.'

She gave a tiny shrug. 'To be honest, I was so young when it all happened that I just grew up with it all. I just accepted that my mum wasn't like other people's—that our lives were different.'

'How did the press never discover that your mother was alive?' he demanded with blatant incredulity. 'How did they never find out about you? You are the only living relatives of one of the richest men on the planet and yet everyone seems unaware of your existence.'

'Like you, they weren't looking,' Alesia said simply. 'We returned to London. My grandfather insisted that my mother reverted to her maiden name and I used the same name. We were called Rawlings. And that was that.'

The beginning of years of hardship that she couldn't even begin to describe.

'That explains why you didn't respond when I addressed you as Philipos at our first meeting,' Sebastien mused. 'Presumably you took that name at your grandfather's insistence?'

Alesia couldn't hide her distaste. 'I *hated* using his name but it was all part of my grandfather's plan to make me seem part of his family,' she said bleakly. 'When you called me Miss Philipos, it used to take me a while to realize that you were talking to me. All my life I'd been Rawlings.'

'Your mother is a brave woman.'

'Don't tell her.' Alesia snatched her hand away from his, her expression urgent. She had to make him understand. 'All her life she has blamed the feud between our two families. We can't tell her I married a Fiorukis; it would kill her.'

His expression didn't alter by so much as a flicker. 'I want you to stop worrying,' he commanded, lounging back in his seat with a complete lack of concern. 'You are looking very pale. You need to rest.'

Alesia wished she could be half as relaxed. Her mind was racing through all the possibilities and none of them seemed attractive. 'I can't rest until we decide what we're going to say to her,' she said breathlessly, her brow lined with worry. 'I didn't know what to say to explain my absence so I told her that I'd taken a job in Greece and—'

He leaned forward in a swift movement, his dark eyes clashing with hers. '*Stop* worrying,' he instructed firmly. 'I will take over from here.'

She chewed on her lower lip. 'But—'

'Rest assured that I will do nothing to hurt your mother further,' he said quietly and she stared at him for a long moment.

'Why would you do that?'

His gaze was suddenly hooded. 'All sorts of reasons,

agape mou. Trust me,' he said quietly. 'And because I have already had ample opportunity to tell your mother the truth.'

It was true. He could have told her mother everything. Instead he'd been calm and reassuring and had revealed nothing that would have caused further upset.

She relaxed back in her seat and closed her eyes. 'I'm sorry.'

'Don't be.' His voice was gruff. 'I understand that you have had to make nothing but difficult decisions from an age when most children were interested in nothing but toys. But you are no longer alone in this, Alesia. The problem is mine. I will deal with it.'

For a moment she felt as though an enormous burden had been lifted from her and then she remembered that he was only doing it because he felt responsible for what had happened. Because the explosion had taken place on his family's boat.

She opened her eyes and glanced at him and then looked away quickly to hide the naked longing that she knew must be visible in her face. Her whole body just *burned* for him. 'Where are we going?'

'My suite at the Dorchester,' he replied tightly, 'where we won't be interrupted. We have rather a lot to talk about, *agape mou*.'

She didn't want to talk.

Wondering how she'd managed to develop into a person who thought about nothing but sex, Alesia crossed her legs to try and relieve the throbbing heat building between her thighs.

'A hotel?' Trying to lighten the tense atmosphere, she managed a smile as she glanced in his direction. 'I've always wanted to order room service. Is it a smart hotel?'

His eyes gleamed with amusement. 'Very,' he replied in his dark drawl. 'It will be another new experience for you. And a new experience for their room service, I suspect.

They've probably never come across anyone with an appetite the size of yours.'

'It's just so nice not to have to economize on food. But I'm actually not that hungry at the moment.' Alesia wondered how anyone could feel sick and starving hungry at the same time.

His sharp gaze was suddenly searching. 'You are still feeling ill? You do look very pale—'

She gave a self-conscious smile. 'It's been a tough day— seeing her lying there in that bed and then you turning up—'

He inhaled deeply. 'I can't believe the sacrifices you made for your mother—'

'She's my only family,' Alesia said simply, turning back to look out of the window again, 'and she made huge sacrifices for me too. She would have preferred me to stay with her but she sent me to boarding school because she thought that would give me my best chance.'

'Your grandfather has a great deal to answer for,' Sebastien said in driven tones and she shrugged helplessly.

'It's just the man he is. He'll never change.'

Sebastien's hard mouth tightened. 'We'll see.'

Their car stopped outside a back entrance to the hotel and within minutes they were inside Sebastien's suite.

Alesia flopped on to one of the beautiful cream sofas in the living area and glanced around her in awe. 'It's amazing—'

'Up until now I've just considered it somewhere to stay when I'm in London,' Sebastien confessed, gesturing towards a phone with a sardonic gleam in his dark eyes. 'Feel free to contact room service. I'm sure they'll appreciate the challenge.'

Her sense of fun flickering to life, Alesia gave a giggle. 'Can I order anything I like?'

'Of course.' He shrugged off his jacket and removed his

tie and their eyes locked, the tension that had been simmering between them suddenly flaring to life.

She could see the hint of dark body hair visible at his throat and the breath jammed in her lungs. 'Sebastien—'

'I promised myself I was going to stay away from you,' he groaned thickly, dragging her to her feet and framing her face with strong hands.

'I don't want you to stay away—' Her heart was thudding against her chest and she gazed into his eyes with something approaching awe. 'I still can't believe it was you. *You saved my life.*'

'A good move on my part,' he murmured, delivering her a sexy smile as he lowered his dark head.

Without lifting his mouth from hers, he stripped her in a few economical movements and lifted her in his arms.

'I can walk—'

'I like to carry you,' he said huskily, his dark head buried in her soft throat as he strode through to the bedroom.

'You mean you like to dominate me,' she teased, gasping as he dropped her on to the bed and came down over her with the arrogant assurance of a man who knew he was irresistible.

'I love the fact that I am the only man who has ever done this to you—' He kissed his way down her helplessly writhing body and proceeded to control her so completely that she lost her ability to think straight.

'Sebastien, please, now—'

He slid a searching, clever finger deep inside her and she arched in shock at his erotic touch.

'You are *so* hot,' he groaned and she whimpered and shifted on the bed in mute desperation.

He continued to drive her wild, to ignore her tiny sobs and moans, subjecting her to almost impossible intimacies until she was totally at the whim of her body.

And when she thought she couldn't stand it any longer he

lifted her and sheathed himself deep inside her with an earthy groan.

Her eyes flew wide and her breathing stopped but then he flashed her a dangerously sexual smile and started to move. With each forceful thrust he drove her higher, capturing her soft gasps with his mouth, urging her forward until she wasn't aware of anything except the explosive excitement building within her own body and his. When her climax hit it was so shockingly good that she clung to him, riding a tidal wave of delicious sensation so powerful that it threatened to engulf her.

He rolled on to his back and took her with him, smoothing her blonde hair away from her face with a gentle hand.

'That was amazing—' he muttered hoarsely. 'The best sex ever.'

Alesia closed her eyes and tried to convince herself that it didn't matter that he didn't love her as long as he wanted her.

Sebastien curved her body against his and then gave a soft curse as his mobile phone rang. 'I left instructions that we were not to be disturbed.'

With barely concealed irritation he reached out a hand and picked up the phone, ending the shrill tone with an impatient stab of his finger.

He listened for several seconds and then said a few words in Greek before severing the connection and inhaling deeply.

'We have to return to the hospital,' he said grimly. 'Apparently your grandfather has decided to pay your mother a visit.'

CHAPTER TEN

WHITE-FACED and anguished, Alesia would have run the length of the corridor that led to her mother's room had Sebastien not caught her arm in a vice-like grip.

'No.' His tone was firm and decisive. 'I know you're worried but I want you to leave this to me.'

Panic in her eyes, Alesia tried to yank her arm away from him. 'You don't understand what he's like. I have to go to her—'

'I understand exactly what he's like,' Sebastien said harshly. 'Trust me when I say that I am better equipped to deal with his particular brand of ruthlessness than you are.'

'But—'

'*Theos mou*, what do I have to do to get you to trust me?' Sebastien growled, jerking her against his hard, muscular body. 'How many times do I have to tell you that I will *not* hurt your mother. But the longer we argue about it, the more damage will be done.'

Alesia felt tears threaten and closed her eyes. 'I didn't know he'd come here,' she whispered and Sebastien's mouth tightened.

'I'm glad he did. It saves me having to go to him although, given the choice, I would have spared your mother this additional stress.' He relaxed his grip on her arm and gave her a smile as breathtakingly sexy as it was unexpected. 'Courage. You have been so brave this far, you can be brave a little longer. And whatever I say, Alesia, I want you to agree with me. Is that clear?'

'Whatever happened to modern?'

He flashed her a smile. 'Gone, but just for today. Do you promise?'

She gave a wan smile in return. 'Has anyone ever told you that you're a bully?'

'Frequently,' he replied calmly. 'Do I have your promise?'

'All right.'

What else could she do?

To her surprise, Sebastien took her hand and escorted her into her mother's room. As she saw the hunched figure of her grandfather Alesia started to shake and she felt Sebastien's hand tighten on hers in silent comfort.

Her mother was lying in the bed, her face white, her eyes fixed on the man who had made her life such a misery.

'I'm astonished that you choose to visit someone whose very existence you have denied,' Sebastien said icily, his dark eyes hard as granite as he surveyed the man standing in front of him with nothing short of contempt.

'It's none of your business,' Dimitrios growled angrily.

Alesia felt her knees quiver but Sebastien's gaze didn't flicker.

'You made it my business when you joined the fortunes of our two families. Let me make something very clear,' he said silkily. 'We have this one conversation and then you are no longer welcome near any member of my family. Particularly my wife and her mother.'

'Ah, yes—how is your *wife*?' The older man gave Alesia a nasty smile. 'I set you up, Fiorukis.'

'And for that I will be eternally grateful.' Sebastien slid a possessive arm around Alesia's waist. 'Had it not been for your relentless scheming, I never would have met Alesia.' He glanced at her briefly and a curious smile touched his firm mouth. 'And that would have been a pity because she has enriched my life.'

Alesia stared at him, momentarily transfixed by the look in his eyes, and then came back down to earth with a bump as Dimitrios Philipos gave a harsh laugh.

'If you're looking at her like that then you obviously haven't seen further than her body. It's time to tell you the truth. She can't give you children. No more Fiorukises.'

Alesia flinched and then felt herself hauled into the protective circle of Sebastien's arms.

'My feelings for Alesia have nothing whatsoever to do with her ability to bear children,' he said, his tone dangerously soft. 'And if you insult my wife one more time you'll regret it, Philipos. Unlike you, I know how to protect my own.'

Alesia held her breath. No one had ever fought in her corner or protected her before. All her life she'd been the one fighting for her mother, she'd been on her own against the world, and then suddenly this man, this man she'd deceived, was standing up for her—

A lump formed in her throat. She loved him so much and she just hated the fact that he felt obliged to look after her.

Lacking her sensibilities, Dimitrios Philipos gave a derisive laugh. 'Face it, Fiorukis, I've won. You may have the company back but you must know by now that nothing can save it and you may pretend that you don't care about children, but we both know the truth about that. You're Greek. Enough said.'

Alesia was frozen to the spot in shock. She stared at Sebastien, waiting to see signs that he was intimidated by the man in front of him, but Sebastien merely studied the older man in grim-faced silence and then, when he finally spoke, his voice was scathing. 'Firstly, the company has been returned to its rightful owner—the Fiorukis family. Your poor business decisions may have virtually brought the company down but my skills will rescue it and rebuild its reputation. As for Alesia—' he tightened his grip on her waist '—she has proved herself to be loyal, strong and loving—the three most important characteristics in a Greek wife.'

Dimitrios gave a snort. 'She can't give you a son and the contract you signed means that you can't get yourself a new wife.'

'Then it's fortunate that I have no desire for a new wife,' Sebastien drawled, his sharp gaze resting on Charlotte's shocked face for a moment before returning to his enemy. 'I think the strain of seeing you has exhausted Alesia's mother. So I want you to leave. Now. It's over. Finished. You are no longer welcome near my family.'

Dimitrios's lip curled. 'They're my family too, Fiorukis. If I choose to stay, I stay.'

'I think not. And it's time to look at some facts.' Sebastien's tone was gritty and hard. 'You lost the right to call them family when you exiled them from Greece and denied their existence. You lost the right to call them family when you failed to offer any provision for them, even though Charlotte's only crime was loving your son. You lost the right to call them family when you shamefully used Alesia as a tool of your own revenge. They are no longer your family, Philipos, *they're mine*.' His dark eyes gave a dangerous flash. 'And I always protect what's mine. Unlike you.'

Dimitrios looked at him warily. 'What's that supposed to mean?'

'You blamed my family for the explosion on our boat,' Sebastien delivered softly, 'but we both know that you—and you alone—arranged that explosion. You were responsible for the death of your own son.'

There was a hideous silence and Alesia heard her mother give a soft gasp of disbelief and shock.

Dimitrios glanced at her, a brief flash of panic in his eyes, and then he turned back to Sebastien, his eyes blazing. 'You think I was trying to kill my own son?'

'No.' Sebastien's gaze was hard. 'I think you were trying to kill my father because he'd been trying to persuade Costas to bury the ridiculous feud between our families once and for all and merge the businesses.'

'It was a ridiculous idea! My son should not have been on that boat!'

Sebastien inhaled sharply. 'The explosion was meant for my family but circumstances changed and when they finally boarded the boat your son and his wife were with them. And it was your son who died along with my uncle. And *you* were responsible. Don't you think it's time to end this feud, Philipos?'

Breathing rapidly, his eyes wild, Dimitrios rushed for the door, but it was blocked by several men.

'The Greek authorities wish to speak to you,' Sebastien said in a tone of utter disgust. 'They're very interested in several events that have taken place, including some of the recent investments you've made.'

Dimitrios paused in the doorway and glared at Sebastien. 'She's going to cost you a fortune.'

At that, Sebastien gave a flicker of a smile. 'I live in hope. I keep giving her my credit card and she refuses to use it. She is utterly unique. Again, I thank you for the introduction. I'd given up hope of ever finding a woman like her.'

As Dimitrios was led from the room Alesia sank on to a chair, her legs shaking too badly to support her weight.

'Is it true?' Charlotte's voice was a croak. '*He* planted the bomb?'

Sebastien nodded, closing the door to ensure privacy. 'We always suspected that he was responsible but there was never any proof.'

'And now?'

Sebastien shrugged. 'There is still very little actual proof, but he has been conducting some extremely shady business deals over the past few years. I think his place of abode for the foreseeable future will be behind bars. Perhaps the reason for putting him there no longer matters.'

Charlotte closed her eyes. 'He is a truly evil man. I think even Costas saw it. It was the reason he wanted to join your father in the business. He wanted a fresh start. I tried to persuade him not to. I was always afraid of what Dimitrios would do. It seems I was right.'

'You paid a high price,' Sebastien agreed quietly and Charlotte's eyes flew open.

'And you paid a high price too. You were forced to marry Alesia in order to return the company to your father.'

Sebastien gave a lopsided smile. 'It was no hardship, I can

assure you,' he drawled softly. 'Your daughter is stunning in every way. Beautiful and brave.'

Charlotte looked at him for a long moment and then turned to Alesia. 'This was the job you mentioned to me? You married for money?'

'There was no other way of getting you the operation,' Alesia said desperately and Sebastien covered her hand with his own.

'She did totally the right thing,' he said smoothly, 'and I would urge that you don't trouble yourself over our relationship. I love your daughter very much and I'm eternally grateful that she chose to marry me.'

Alesia shot him a grateful look. Even though she knew he was just protecting her mother from the truth, even though she knew he didn't really love her—

'And now you must rest.' Sebastien straightened in a lithe movement and glanced towards the door, where a doctor was hovering. 'I understand that you have made improvements today. I want you to know that as soon as you are well enough I intend to fly you to my home in Athens. Sunshine can be very restorative and you don't see enough of it in London.'

'Greece?' Charlotte gave a tremulous smile. 'I never thought to see Greece again, even though it was once my home—'

In a gesture that surprised Alesia, Sebastien stooped to kiss her forehead. 'And, rest assured, it will be your home again.'

Back in the hotel, Alesia collapsed on the white sofa feeling utterly drained. Her head swam and she felt totally washed out. 'Thank you,' she said hoarsely. 'For all the things you said to her, thank you. And for standing up to my grandfather. I suspect you're the only person to ever do that.'

'We are well rid of him,' Sebastien said, dark eyes surveying her with visible concern. 'You look on the point of collapse. I should *not* have taken you with me. It was too much for you.'

'I'm fine,' Alesia muttered, rubbing fingers across her forehead. 'Just tired, I suppose.'

Sebastien gave a brief nod. 'Eat something,' he ordered roughly, 'and then you can sleep.'

He reached for the phone to order room service just as Alesia stood up to use the bathroom.

Immediately she felt blackness descend on her and slid to the floor in a heap.

She awoke to find Sebastien on his knees beside her, his powerful frame simmering with pulsing tension, his jaw clenched hard as he held her hand and tried to revive her.

As her eyes flickered open he released a juddering breath. '*When* are you going to stop doing this to me? I never knew the meaning of the word fear until I met you.'

She closed her eyes again, wishing that the feeling of sickness would pass. 'Sorry,' she mumbled weakly. 'I don't know what's wrong with me—'

'I do,' Sebastien contradicted her in a grim tone. 'You have been under severe strain. Starting with the wedding, then worry about your mother, followed by a traumatic experience in my pool and then the stress of having the truth discovered. Then meeting your grandfather again.'

Alesia squeezed her eyes tightly shut, unable to look at him. 'Don't remind me. My grandfather tried to kill your family. You saved my life and my mother's life and I repay you by forcing you to marry me, even though I can't give you the children I know you want. I feel *so* guilty.' She covered her face with her hands and gave a soft groan, just tortured by the enormity of everything that had happened. 'Do other people have lives as complex as mine?'

'Possibly not,' he drawled, a hint of humour in his dark tone. 'But I'm sure their lives would be very boring by comparison.'

She shook her head, utterly swamped by guilt and unable to raise a laugh. Her hands dropped to her sides and she forced herself to look at him. 'I never intended to marry anyone, you know. I decided that it wouldn't be fair.'

Sebastien inhaled sharply. 'Presumably that's why you were still a virgin on our wedding night?'

Alesia nodded. 'I never let men get close. I didn't want to risk becoming attached to any of them.'

'But marrying me was easy because you hated me so much,' Sebastien said wryly. 'You blamed me for everything.'

'It was the wrong thing to do,' she groaned in mortified tones. 'I see that now. But I was desperate for the money and I couldn't see any other way of getting it. And I didn't have all the facts—' The room started to swim again and she lay back against the cushions of the sofa, her face ashen.

'Neither of us had all the facts, *agape mou*,' Sebastien said quietly, his eyes clouded with worry as he looked at her, 'but now we do. Stop worrying. You're making yourself ill. The doctor will be here in a minute.'

'It's probably nothing,' Alesia mumbled, placing a hand on her churning stomach. 'I just picked up a bug when I swallowed all that water.'

'Well, whatever it is I want it sorted out,' Sebastien growled and Alesia almost smiled at that. The doctor had better have an instant diagnosis to hand; otherwise he was going to experience Sebastien's legendary lack of tolerance.

There was a knock on the door and one of the Fiorukis security team entered with a tall man who Alesia assumed to be the doctor. Under Sebastien's eagle eye he asked her all sorts of detailed questions, some of them more than a little embarrassing, but Sebastien didn't flicker an eyelid, his expression grim and expectant as he watched the doctor.

Finally the other man straightened and closed his bag. 'How long have you been married?'

'Six weeks.'

'Then I think congratulations are in order,' he said lightly. 'You're going to have a baby.'

There was a hideous silence and finally Alesia found her voice. 'But that isn't possible,' she croaked and the doctor gave a wry smile.

'After what you've told me about your medical history I can understand why you'd think that, but I can absolutely assure you that you are pregnant, Mrs Fiorukis.'

'But—'

'I've been a doctor for thirty years,' the doctor said calmly, 'and, although every doctor is occasionally in doubt about a diagnosis, this time I'm completely sure. The sickness you've been experiencing is a normal part of pregnancy. It should pass in a few weeks' time, as will the tiredness. Hopefully then you'll be able to enjoy the experience.'

Alesia didn't dare breathe. She was *pregnant*?

Sebastien raked long fingers through his dark hair, a stunned expression in his eyes. 'But how could the other doctors have got it so wrong?'

The doctor shrugged and walked towards the door. 'There is much that we understand about fertility and conception but equally there is much that we don't understand,' he admitted. 'Why else do desperate couples adopt, only to produce a child naturally? I have seen men with virtually no sperm count succeed in fathering a child. Although we doctors like to pretend that we have all the answers, the truth is that nature can sometimes produce miracles. You've just experienced that miracle, Mr Fiorukis. Be grateful.'

Sebastien closed the door behind the doctor and walked back to Alesia, who was still lying on the sofa.

'I'm afraid to move,' she whispered and he gave a wry smile of understanding.

'I don't think it will fall out,' he said huskily, scooping her up in his arms and carrying her into the bedroom.

'What are you doing?'

'Getting you the rest you badly need.'

She closed her eyes. There was still so much that needed to be said. 'Do you realize what this means?'

He tensed slightly as he lowered her gently into the middle of the bed. 'What does this mean?'

'We are now allowed to divorce.'

He stilled and then he stretched out a lean bronzed hand

to flick off the light. 'Go to sleep,' he said, strain thickening his deep drawl, 'and we'll talk in the morning.'

Alesia closed her eyes to hold back the tears that threatened to give her away. She was pregnant. She was having a baby. She ought to be filled with joy.

So why did her life suddenly seem so empty?

When Alesia awoke it was daylight and Sebastien was sprawled in a chair in the corner of the room, watching her through veiled eyes.

'Sebastien?' She struggled upright. 'What are you doing there?'

'I didn't trust you not to do one of your disappearing acts,' he said gruffly, running a hand over his roughened jaw, 'and you're not going anywhere until we've had a conversation. Stay there and don't move.'

He left the room and returned moments later carrying a plate of biscuits and a drink.

She sat up and looked at him quizzically. 'What's this?'

'The doctor suggested that dry biscuits before you move in the morning might help the sickness,' he said, the strain of the past few days visible in his face. He waited while she nibbled the biscuit. 'Is that better?'

She chewed and then nodded. 'Yes, actually, it is.'

'Good.' He inhaled deeply and then sat on the edge of the bed. 'Because we need to talk and I don't want you finding excuses to leave the room. And before you speak another word, there is one thing you should know. I am willing to agree to almost anything you ask, but I will not give you a divorce. So don't ever ask me again.'

Alesia put the half-eaten biscuit back on the plate. 'You're not responsible for what happened, Sebastien. I know that now. It was all my grandfather's fault. I wonder if that is part of the reason he couldn't bear to have my mother and me in his life? Perhaps it intensified his guilt, reminding him of what he'd done.'

'You assume that he is capable of guilt and remorse,'

Sebastien muttered, 'but frankly I'm not so sure. And the reason I don't want you to leave has nothing to do with my own feelings of responsibility and everything to do with the way I feel about *you*.'

Alesia gave a wobbly smile. He was Greek to the very backbone. He'd fathered a child and his traditional macho instincts wouldn't allow him to let her go, even though he didn't love her.

'This is just because you know I'm pregnant—'

'The way I feel about you has nothing to do with the fact that you're pregnant,' he groaned. 'Although I can't pretend I'm not delighted about that because it ties you to me. I cannot believe that a woman as loyal and giving as you would willingly deprive her child of a father.'

She closed her eyes. 'Sebastien, this is ridiculous. You made it perfectly clear what you thought of me right from the beginning. You thought I was the very worst type of gold-digger, and in a way I *was*—'

'That was before I knew you,' he breathed, the skin stretched taut over his hard bone structure. 'And I feel *very* guilty about the way I treated you.'

'I don't blame you for any of that—'

'Then you should,' he said roughly, removing the tray from her lap and putting it on a nearby table. 'You seem to have forgotten that I'm not exactly blameless. 'You were forced to marry me for money but I just assumed you were like all the other women I'd ever known and I treated you abominably.'

'Sebastien—'

'But you have to understand that I'd never met a woman like you before,' he groaned as he came down beside her on the bed. 'All the women I've met in the past have only ever been interested in material things. I assumed that was why you wanted the money.'

She opened her eyes and gave a faint smile at that. 'I can't pretend I don't enjoy being able to wear nice things and eat delicious food—'

'Then stay with me and I will teach you how your sex is supposed to behave,' he said with a sardonic smile that wasn't quite steady. 'I'll teach you how to spend, spend, spend and party, party, party. You deserve it.'

It was so tempting just to say yes. 'It isn't enough, Sebastien,' she said shakily, lifting a hand to her throbbing head. 'You'll get bored.'

'Never—you constantly surprise me—'

'You've never stayed with one woman for more than five minutes—'

'And with you I can't be away from you even for that long,' he pointed out in husky tones. 'Or has that fact escaped you?'

She blushed. 'That's just sex.'

'*Not* just sex,' he contradicted her, inhaling deeply as if he were bracing himself to say something. 'I love you and I know that you don't feel the same way about me, but I still can't let you go.'

She stilled. 'You don't love me—you just said that for the benefit of my mother and grandfather.'

'I said it because it is true,' he said quietly, stroking a hand over her tumbled hair and giving her a strangely uncertain smile. 'I never thought love existed before I met you and now I've found it I can't let it go, even though I know it isn't reciprocated. I still think I can make you happy.'

Alesia was in a daze. He *loved* her? 'You can't possibly love me—after our wedding night you just walked out. You didn't even spend the night with me.'

'Don't remind me what a total louse I was,' he groaned, sliding his hands around her face and forcing her to look at him. 'I was so cruel to you.'

'Because you hated me—'

'Because I didn't trust myself in the bed with you,' he corrected her, bringing his mouth down on her softy parted lips and stealing a drugging kiss. 'It took a monumental effort on my part not to climb back into bed with you and make love until you couldn't move.'

'Then why didn't you?'

'Because what I felt for you scared me and I didn't like feeling that way,' he confessed with unusual candour. 'You made me feel out of control and I just hated that. Particularly given the sort of woman I believed you to be.'

'So you vanished for two weeks without any contact—'

He gave a rueful smile. 'I wasn't used to being faced with powerful emotions because it had never happened to me before. I decided to keep my distance and on top of that I was working twenty-four hours a day trying to unravel the mess your grandfather had made of the company.'

She stared at him. It hadn't occurred to her that he'd been under pressure at work but of course he must have been. 'We were so close on the island but after I told you that I was infertile you didn't come near me. I thought you *hated* me.'

'At first I was angry,' he conceded, sliding an arm round her and tucking her against him, 'but when I calmed down I realized that you'd had no choice but to marry me. Because of the person that you are and because of your circumstances, you made the only decision open to you. Once I recognized that, I didn't want you to be forced to endure my company.'

'But you announced that you were going to continue to support me because you felt responsible for the explosion even though you weren't even there.'

He sighed. 'I'd sensed trouble all along. I'd advised my father not to have the meeting because I didn't trust your grandfather not to intervene. But he thought it was time to mend fences and I was only nineteen—why should he listen to me? I was arrogant—thought I knew everything—'

Alesia looked up at him. 'But you were *right*.'

He shrugged. 'As it turns out, yes. I decided to go to the meeting anyway but, as I reached the bay, the boat exploded. In the chaos afterwards I never knew who was on board.'

Her gaze softened. 'I still can't believe it was you who saved me—'

'It was fate,' he growled possessively, tightening his grip on her. 'You were meant to be mine all along.'

'That's guilt, Sebastien,' she whispered, 'not love, and you have no reason to feel responsible for what happened.'

'It's *not* guilt,' he said fiercely, 'and one day I will make you love me the way I love you.'

The breath jammed in her throat. 'Do you mean it?'

'I am devoting every waking hour to finding ways of making you love me,' he vowed and she shook her head, her gaze suddenly shy as she stared up at him.

'No, I mean do you really love me?'

'You need more convincing?' He gave a wry smile. 'I have made myself vulnerable for the first time in my life, *agape mou*, and for a very proud Greek man, that should say it all. The fact that I'm prepared to confess my love, knowing that it isn't returned—'

'It is returned. I do love you, Sebastien,' she whispered softly, her blue eyes reflecting everything she felt. 'I've loved you from the moment I realized what sort of man you really are. Strong, dependable, responsible. Everything that my grandfather isn't.'

His powerful body tensed and he stared at her intently. 'You don't have to lie to me to make me feel better—'

She shook her head. 'No more lies, ever. From now on, only the truth and the truth is that I love you.'

He caught the words in his mouth and kissed her. 'Tell me again,' he groaned against her mouth, 'and again—'

'I love you.' Alesia gave a womanly smile and then gasped as his mouth found a sensitive spot at the base of her neck. 'Oh, Sebastien—'

'No other man is ever going to discover just how hot you are,' he vowed, pulling her down next to him and curving her trembling body into his.

'I forgot to add that as well as strong, dependable and responsible, you're also macho, overbearing and impossibly possessive,' she teased, and he gave a smug smile.

'I'm Greek, *agape mou*. What do you expect?'

'I like the fact that you want to protect me. No one has ever done that for me before.'

He tightened his hold on her. 'From now on, *nothing* will hurt you. And we need never go to the island again,' he promised her in thickened tones. 'We can live in cities if that is where you feel more comfortable.'

'I don't mind where we live as long as you're there,' she confessed breathlessly, snuggling against him like a contented kitten. 'You make me feel safe. I don't think swimming in the sea will ever be my speciality but I can learn to fly over it as long as you're holding my hand. I love the island, Sebastien. It's the place where I fell in love with you.'

He gave a groan and dropped a kiss on the top of her head. 'We will find the very best counsellors to cure you of your fear of water and I'm never letting you out of my sight again, *agape mou*,' he vowed huskily. 'From now on you're mine and I *always* protect what is mine. Anything you want, you have only to ask.'

'Anything?' Her eyes twinkled and he gave an appreciative laugh.

'Now you're making me nervous.' His wickedly sexy eyes gleamed. 'What is it you want? At this point perhaps I ought to warn you that I won't permit the mother of my child to walk around dressed in a miniskirt and three-inch heels.'

'Possessive again,' she teased, but her arms slid round the strong column of his neck and she pressed a kiss into the corner of his mouth. 'Did you mean what you said about my mother living in Greece?'

'Of course. The doctors feel she will recuperate much faster in the sunshine,' he told her. 'As soon as she is well enough to travel we will have her transferred to a private hospital in Athens.'

Alesia sighed. 'What it is to have money—'

'You still have to ask me for something for yourself,' he reminded her, a trace of amusement lighting his dark gaze.

'What are you, the genie of the lamp?'

He gave a groan of submission. 'I just want to give you everything,' he confessed and she smiled the smile of a woman who knew she was truly loved.

'In that case, can we go back to Greece as soon as possible? I'm in love with Greek food and Greek sunshine.'

'And Greek men?' He dropped a kiss on her parted lips. 'Are you in love with them also?'

'Just the one Greek man, Mr Fiorukis,' she replied with a laugh in her eyes. 'Just the one.'

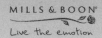

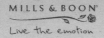

researching the cure

The facts you need to know:

- **One woman in nine** in the United Kingdom will develop breast cancer during her lifetime.

- Each year **40,700** women are newly diagnosed with breast cancer and around **12,800** women will die from the disease. However, survival rates are improving, with on average 77 per cent of women still alive five years later.

- **Men can also suffer from breast cancer**, although currently they make up less than one per cent of all new cases of the disease.

Britain has one of the highest breast cancer death rates in the world. Breast Cancer Campaign wants to understand why and do something about it. Statistics cannot begin to describe the impact that breast cancer has on the lives of those women who are affected by it and on their families and friends.

4 FREE

BOOKS AND A SURPRISE GIFT!

We would like to take this opportunity to thank you for reading this Mills & Boon® book by offering you the chance to take FOUR more specially selected titles from the Modern Romance™ series absolutely FREE! We're also making this offer to introduce you to the benefits of the Reader Service™—

- ★ **FREE home delivery**
- ★ **FREE gifts and competitions**
- ★ **FREE monthly Newsletter**
- ★ **Exclusive Reader Service offers**
- ★ **Books available before they're in the shops**

Accepting these FREE books and gift places you under no obligation to buy, you may cancel at any time, even after receiving your free shipment. Simply complete your details below and return the entire page to the address below. You don't even need a stamp!

YES! Please send me 4 free Modern Romance books and a surprise gift. I understand that unless you hear from me, I will receive 6 superb new titles every month for just £2.75 each, postage and packing free. I am under no obligation to purchase any books and may cancel my subscription at any time. The free books and gift will be mine to keep in any case.

P5ZED

Ms/Mrs/Miss/Mr ....Initials ....
BLOCK CAPITALS PLEASE

Surname ....

Address ....

....

....Postcode...

Send this whole page to:
UK: FREEPOST CN81, Croydon, CR9 3WZ